ABIGAIL

A Scandalous Suffragette Novel

BY SYLVIA MCDANIEL

Books by Sylvia McDaniel

Contemporary Romance

Standalones
The Reluctant Santa
My Sister's Boyfriend
The Wanted Bride
The Relationship Coach
Her Christmas Lie
Secrets, Lies, and Online Dating
Paying for the Past
Cupid's Revenge

Anthologies
Kisses, Laughter & Love
Christmas with you

Collaborative Series

Magic, New Mexico
Touch of Decadence

Western Historicals

Standalones
A Hero's Heart
A Scarlet Bride
Second Chance Cowboy

The Cuvier Women
Wronged
Betrayed
Beguiled

Lipstick and Lead
Desperate
Deadly
Dangerous
Daring
Determined
Deceived

Scandalous Suffragettes
Abigail
Bella
Callie
Faith

The Burnett Brides
The Rancher Takes a Bride
The Outlaw Takes a Bride
The Marshal Takes a Bride
The Christmas Bride

Anthologies
Wild Western Women
Courting the West
Wild Western Women Ride Again

Collaborative Series

The Surprise Brides
Ethan

American Mail Order Brides
Katie

Abigail: Scandalous Suffragette
Published by Virtual Bookseller: July 2015

Cover Design by Kim Killion
http://thekilliongroupinc.com/

Edited by Tina Winograd
www.tinaeditservices.com

Formatted by Laurelle Procter
laurelleprocter@gmail.com

Short Description: This little rebel is determined to bring the town's laws into the nineteenth century, even if it means sacrificing her reputation.

ISBN: 978-1-942608-58-5 (paperback)
ISBN: 978-1-942608-02-8 (e-book)

{Historical Victorian Romance – Fiction}

www.SylviaMcDaniel.com

Synopsis

In New Hope, Texas women like children, are to be seen and not heard. Their only job in life is to marry, procreate, and be a loyal, obedient wife. Thus the shortage of available women. Until, Abigail Vanderhooten is unexpectedly called home, her head filled with ideas of changing the world where a woman can own a business and have a bank account. This little rebel is determined to bring the town's laws into the nineteenth century, even if it means sacrificing her reputation.

Jack Turner likes being the mayor in a small, quiet western town where the biggest rabble rousers are cowboys on Saturday night. Everything is about to change when Abigail Vanderhooten, a tiny sprite of a woman returns to town, ready to take on the local laws. While trying to keep the town from splitting apart, he's surprised how her strong spirit captivates him. And he's shocked when she manages to worm her way into his bachelor heart, with her controversial ideas of women earning a living the same as a man.

With a woman's revolution brewing, will Jack be forced to run her out of town, before he has a chance to convey how she's changed him? Or will Abigail give up on New Hope, Texas and return to Boston?

Can love blossom and change a woman and a man with different ideals?

Table of Contents

Chapter One

Abigail Vanderhooten wasn't a thief, a prostitute, a murderer, or a cheat. But here she sat with all of her friends in the Boston city jail. What was their crime? Being a woman!

Women had so few rights. No bank accounts, no land, and no vote. And owning a business was frowned upon in many cities and outlawed in others. Their sole purpose in life was to become a wife and mother. Marry, procreate, and make their husband look good. Sit down, shut-up, and look pretty.

Well, Abigail and her friends wanted more. Much more and after attending Matilda Joslyn Gage's speech at the National Women's Suffrage Association's convention, they'd made a commitment *to change* the world.

Except, they'd hit a small snag. The Boston city police took exception to them blocking the entrance to one of the local banks. And now here they were waiting in jail.

"Abigail, I want to draw attention to a woman's plight, but I'm not certain my daddy is going to keep paying for me to attend Boston University if I keep getting thrown in jail. If my mother finds out, she's going to take a switch to my hide," Callie said, shifting on the hard wooden floor.

The cell held nothing more than one cot, a slop jar, and the eight of them. They'd been in here since yesterday afternoon, and they were exhausted, hungry, and so ready to go back to their dorms.

"Callie, we must all make sacrifices to bring about a difference."

Faith leaned back against the wall and crossed her arms over her chest. "Maybe we're going about this wrong. Maybe we should start our own town."

"Which one of us is going to construct the buildings?"

Bella asked.

Abigail sighed and thought about Faith's idea. Maybe it would be simpler to just start fresh somewhere and make up their own laws. Their chances of getting what they needed would be a lot easier. "There are going to be things we don't have the strength to do, but we hire men for what we need that we can't provide. Being an independent woman doesn't mean we don't need men. We just want more control over our own destiny."

"Good, because I kind of like men," Diamond said with a giggle, pushing back her red hair. The most beautiful of them all, she said her stage actress mother had named her daughter after her favorite jewel her most recent suitor had given her.

"Oh dear," Emma said, shaking her head. "You've lost the spirit of the movement. We're learning to be independent from men and playing kissy face with them does not help the cause."

Abigail sat back and looked at each of her friends. "Tell me what you would do if we did build our own town? And what would bring families and men to this town?"

"I'd be a baker," Bella said. "You know how much I love to bake."

"I think I gained ten pounds off that last batch of crumpets you made. Gosh, those were good. But that's a woman's job," Georgia said. "I'm hungry."

Abigail nodded her head, agreeing with her friend. But they had to have bigger ambitions.

"I don't know. I just don't want to do what my mother has done all her life. Do you know what it's like for a woman who has nine kids in twelve years?" Haley said softly.

An only child, Abigail would have liked to have had more brothers and sisters. It was just her and her father, since her mother died when she was twelve. And then her father, at her mother's insistence, had sent her back East for her education on how to be a proper young woman.

Wouldn't he be shocked to learn she was in jail for protesting the banks' regulations regarding women?

"Me, I'd like to be a doctor. I'm going to help women by studying how to keep from getting pregnant. Having a baby every two to three years kills a lot of women," Emma replied.

Of all the girls, besides Abigail, in this march to liberate women, Emma was the smartest, and she would graduate from the university at the end of the month. Someday, she would be an excellent healer, and already, she was working with the national organization, talking to women about how not to conceive a baby every nine months.

Quiet, shy Callie lifted her head and glanced at each of them. "I want to open a bank. Give women bank accounts and loan them money. I would advance each of you whatever it was you needed to start your business."

Diamond, the most flamboyant one of the group, laughed. "I just want to have fun. If I can have fun and run a business, I will. If not, then I'm going to find a way. I'm tired of all this seriousness. Yes, I want to help women, but sitting here inside a jail cell is not my idea of a good time."

Abigail's mother would have considered Diamond to be an improper young woman. But Abigail knew that beneath all the flash and flamboyant speech was a scared girl afraid of returning to her mother.

"Maybe you need to open a saloon," Faith said, and they knew she was being facetious.

"Maybe I will. I could sing and maybe even dance," Diamond said. "I just don't want to go back to my family and watch my mother entertain her newest gentleman friend."

The sound of a door opening made Abigail glance up

from the floor, where they were all sitting. She watched as a policeman approached the cell.

"Ladies, I'm going to let you go with a warning. Any other demonstrations will result in fines. Are we clear?"

Clear as mud was the response Abigail wanted to declare, but she was ready to get out of this cell. Sitting on a wooden floor was not her idea of luxury.

"Mrs. Minor is vouching for you, and I've agreed to let you go in her custody. No more demonstrations."

"I thought we lived in America, the land of the free," Emma said.

The policeman frowned. "These are my terms. You can accept them or stay in jail, and I'll telegraph each one of your families. Your choice."

"Abigail, I can't have my papa finding out we went to jail," Bella said.

Bella's father was searching for a suitable match for her—a man who would increase the family's financial empire. Abigail thought he should just hang a price tag around his daughter's neck. The result would be the same.

These ladies were all fighting not only for their independence, but the right to choose and marry a man they were in love with. Not a man who would elevate their financial status in the world.

"I want to go back to our dorm," Faith said quietly. "I'm tired."

"Let's not concede defeat. Let's stay and fight," Diamond replied.

Just then, Mrs. Minor stepped into the jail area. "Girls, it's time to give up." She waved an envelope. "Abigail, I have a telegram for you from home."

"Ladies, before I open this door, I need you to tell me you understand. No more protests or I will fine you so badly you'll have to contact your families to get out of jail."

"Oh, all right," Abigail said, a trickle of worry scurrying along her spine like a rat deserting a sinking ship. "I need to read that message."

"Now, ladies, no more trouble. Boston has had enough of you." The officer opened the jail door with a clang.

Abigail rushed to Mrs. Minor, and she handed over the telegram.

COME HOME. YOUR FATHER IS ILL.

A pang zipped through Abigail's body, and her chest clenched with pain. He must be bad if they'd sent for her. She knew what she had to do.

"Ladies, my father is ill. I'm catching the next train to Fort Worth."

~

As the stage pulled in to New Hope, Texas, Abigail noted how the small town set on the edge of the prairie had changed. Wooden sidewalks were filled with people and the streets were congested with wagons, but other than that it didn't look much different than when her father had sent her away to school when she was barely twelve.

Oh God, she remembered begging him not to make her go, but he'd made a promise to her mother on her death bed that Abigail would receive the proper education of a young woman. And he'd sent her to Boston to the school her mother had attended when she'd been a girl.

But how had it helped Abigail's mother? She'd married a man who'd taken her to a ruthless frontier town. Where the men ran the town and the women were seen and not heard. Well, Abigail required more out of life than what her mother had wanted.

When the stage came to a halt, Abigail opened the door and stepped down. It had taken her two weeks to reach the West from Boston. She felt tired and dusty and just wanted to see her father and rest.

"Miss Vanderhooten?" a tall handsome man asked.

The very sight of the brawny cowboy made her breath catch. She didn't know who he was, but he was more attractive than any of the boys in college with his sandy blond hair, large hazel eyes framed with long dark lashes, and a full sensuous mouth.

"Yes, sir," she said curtly. Gorgeous men left her feeling gangly and awkward and she was no longer charmed by their persuasive behavior.

The man reached out his hand. "Jack Turner. Your father sent me to meet your stage. Welcome home to New Hope."

"Thank you," she said, glancing around as boisterous music blasted from the end of the street. "Is there some sort of celebration going on?" she asked, searching for the source of the music.

Jack smiled. "No, that's the saloon."

She shook her head. That was a typical saloon, cranking out music probably at all hours of the day and night. "Doesn't the city have some kind of ordinance against making noise all hours of the day and night?"

"No, miss."

"Are you sure? Good grief, I would be contacting the mayor, complaining about the volume of the music. Even in Boston, our saloons weren't allowed to be that loud."

"I'll let the mayor know," he said.

"You do that," she said, feeling put out and cranky. She was hot, dusty, and dirty, and the clothes she was wearing had been perfectly fine in Boston, but here, the extra layers were making her skin sizzle and sweat like she was in a sauna.

She sighed. She was home, yet somehow, she felt like she'd left civilization.

Mr. Turner had the station men load her trunk in his wagon. Then he placed his hands on her waist and lifted her into the wooden contraption before she could utter a word of protest.

"Mr. Turner, you're being presumptuous."

He turned and stared at her in surprise. "Excuse me?"

"Placing your hands on me and lifting me into the wagon."

Hazel eyes stared at her like she had no sense. He gave her a charming smile. "How else were you going to get in the wagon? That skirt of yours is fitting, and that bustle would probably have you falling over backwards. I was trying to help you."

She glanced over the side of the wagon and noticed the ground was a ways down, and she would have had a hard time crawling up in her traveling dress.

"Oh," she said, feeling a bit of embarrassment. Suddenly, she realized life was a lot different in New Hope from Boston. There, the carriages were made for women to crawl into, not so here. But, she was an independent woman—a lady who didn't require a man. "Well, I didn't need your help."

"Good, I won't help you down," he said clearly put out with her.

Abigail almost fell out of the wagon as he clicked to the horses. With a lurch, the wagon took off down the street.

"Oh dear," she said, hanging on tightly to the sides of the wagon.

"I guess they don't have wagons up in Boston?"

"No, sir. They have carriages, which are much lower to the ground. A lady can get in and out on her own without the help of a man."

He frowned at her and then returned his gaze to the road in front of him.

"I could have walked."

A chuckle escaped him. "No, I don't think so. Your papa would have been most upset if his daughter had not been met at the station. Besides, it's a good half mile, and in this heat that would have certainly worn you out."

"I'm not so fragile that the heat would wilt me."

A grin spread across his face. "Miss, not to be disagreeable, but you're dressed like a blue norther is about to hit in the middle of June."

Abigail wasn't certain what a blue norther was, but she did feel like she was slowly cooking under all these clothes. Back home, she would have been perfectly fine, but here, the temperature was quite a bit warmer.

"I'd suggest maybe removing some of those layers of clothing, including that petticoat," he said with a smile. "You'll be a lot cooler."

Abigail bristled. "You, sir, are entirely too forward. The nerve of talking to me about my petticoats."

The man shook his head. "Fine. But when you faint from the heat, I'm going to say I told you so."

Sure, she could remember the warmer temperatures from when she was a young girl, but that had been over six years ago. And she hadn't known what to expect on the journey home.

They arrived at the mercantile, and she glanced up at the building. It looked the same, yet not as large as she remembered. The paint was faded on the outside of the building, the wood worn and bleached from the sun.

Jack jumped down from the wagon and secured the horses. He walked around to her side, paused for just a second, and then continued on. The silly man wasn't going to help her alight from the wagon, and she had brought his rudeness upon herself.

She grasped the side and swung her leg over, trying to find the ground. It wasn't like she could jump with her bustle; it made it difficult to get enough width to spread her legs and climb down.

Jack carried her trunk into the building and then came

out again. She was still sitting in the wagon.

"I'm stuck. I can't reach the ground."

"Oh my, you're in quite a pickle. I don't want to be too forward and place my hands on your person without your permission. How are you going to get down?" He stood there, his arms crossed, his legs planted firmly like a tree sprouting roots. Not moving, waiting for her to grovel.

She glared at him. "You've made your point, Mr. Turner. Would you please help me out of the wagon?"

He laughed and walked over to the side of the vehicle, placed his hands beneath her knees and back, and scooped her out of the wagon.

She gasped with indignation. This was even more personal than if he'd touched her waist. "Mr. Turner, my father will be outraged."

"Yes, Miss Vanderhooten," he said with a smile, his lips mere inches from hers.

While she was frustrated as hell with the man, she had a sudden urge to touch his mouth, run her fingertips across those full lips, and maybe even kiss the man. She'd only kissed two boys in her life, and both had been so sloppy she'd never gone out with the men again.

He dropped his hand from beneath her knees and let her body slide down the front of him, a wicked grin on his handsome face. Abigail could feel the heat spread across her cheeks, with the shame of what he'd done, on a public street no less.

"Now, that was what is considered being touched inappropriately by a man. But I must admit, I enjoyed every second. In the West, I would suggest you let a man help you in and out of the wagon, Miss Vanderhooten."

"Hrmph! Thank you, sir, but you are no gentleman."

Laughter bellowed from his chest. "Never pretended to be one. Now, let's get you inside and check on your papa." Jack opened the door and waited for her to enter.

Hot and flustered even more than when she'd gotten off the stage, she rushed through the door, hoping to see her papa and find out this was all a huge mistake. That the urgent telegram she'd received was a joke.

She glanced around the store and noticed nothing had changed since she was a little girl—the same displays, the same canned and sacked items in the same places. The store actually looked old and run down. Nothing like what she'd seen in Boston.

"Who are you?" she asked the man behind the counter.

"Don Martin," he said. "And you?"

"I'm Abigail Vanderhooten."

Jack followed her through the door. "Hi, Don."

"Jack," the man responded as he came around the counter and gripped her hand. "We've been expecting you, Miss Vanderhooten. It's nice to meet you finally. I've been watching the store for your father."

"Thank you," she said. "How is Papa?"

A frown came over his face. "I'll let him tell you. He's upstairs."

"Thanks. I'll go up now and say hello."

"Of course," he said, his face not registering any warmth.

"I'm leaving, Miss Vanderhooten," Jack said with a wink. "It was a pleasure meeting you. I'm sure we'll cross paths again, very soon."

It was on the tip of her tongue to say, not if she could help it, but then thought better. No sense in making an enemy the first hour she was in town. For all she knew, Jack could be her father's friend.

"I'm sure," she said and bit her lip, not wanting to say the words, but knowing she must. "Thank you for picking me up."

He grinned like he knew how much it cost her to say those words. The man was an arrogant, overbearing bore, a typical man.

"You're quite welcome. The pleasure was mine," he said, and she knew he was being sarcastic.

"Yes, it was," she said, referring to his improper display on the street.

Turning away from him, Abigail hurried up the stairs. Time to put meeting that bore of a man who had picked her up at the station behind her and concentrate on seeing her father.

When she reached the second floor, she heard the sound of someone wheezing, struggling to breathe. That couldn't be Papa, could it?

She slowly walked around the corner and saw a frail thin man lying in the bed, struggling with each breath. A woman sat beside his bed, holding his hand.

The lady jumped up when she saw Abigail. "Praise God, you're here."

Abigail glanced down at the obviously decaying body. "Oh, Papa. Why didn't you tell me you were so sick?"

"You're all grown up," he wheezed, ignoring her comment.

Reaching down, she hugged the bones that were all that was left of her papa.

"Why isn't he getting any better?" she asked the woman.

She shook her head. "He has consumption."

Abigail's heart sank. She knew the disease was a death sentence. That it was only a matter of time.

Her father clasped her hand. "I had to see you again, to know you would be all right. It won't be long now."

"I'm here, Papa." Tears clogged her throat, making it difficult to speak, but she knew she couldn't let him see her cry. She just couldn't break down in front of him. It would only make him feel bad, and she wanted whatever time they had left together to be happy.

The woman motioned for her to sit beside him, and Abigail took the chair.

"You look like your mother," he said. "How was that fancy college?"

"It was fine, Papa. I'm three years away from getting my business degree. Your daughter is going to be one of the few women graduates."

He smiled. "You're just as headstrong as your mother."

"Now, Papa," she said, "I'm not headstrong. I'm independent."

He tried to laugh, but instead, he gurgled. "We need to talk about what you should do when I'm gone."

She frowned. "Let's not talk about you dying. Let's get you well."

"Honey, it's my time. I'm just happy I got to see you again."

"Well, I'm home now. So, we're going to do everything we can to get you better."

He smiled, a sad expression on his face. "I wish it were possible. I really do, but my time has come."

Later the next day, Abigail watched the life drain out of her father's body. She'd barely made it home before he was gone.

~

On the day of the funeral, Abigail struggled to keep her composure. The entire town turned out in honor of Walter Vanderhooten. The local women fussed over Abigail as if they wanted to protect her from the grief that consumed her. Frankly, she wanted everyone to go home and let her mourn in private for her last family member. Numb, she realized she was all alone in the world.

She remembered her mother's funeral and realized nothing had changed. The men attended out of respect, while the women arranged for food, comforted her, and helped with the details. Women were the healers, while the men were the shakers and movers. But when it came to emotional matters, the men shut down and let the women handle the caring for the living.

All she had to do was get through the luncheon, and then she'd be free to rest and spend five minutes alone to contemplate her future, to privately grieve her father.

"Excuse me, Miss Vanderhooten," a tall man said, touching her arm. "I wanted to give you my condolences regarding your father. I also wanted to let you know I would very much be interested in purchasing the mercantile from you."

Abigail stopped and stared at the man. "Who said I was going to sell the mercantile?"

Until this moment, the store had been the last thing on her mind. She didn't know what she was going to do with the business she'd grown up watching her mother and father struggle over—the place where she'd watched her father hand out free food to people he knew were starving or had children at home who were hungry. Or the time the freight drivers had all gone on strike, and her father had driven an empty wagon to Fort Worth to pick up their stock.

Part of her wasn't interested in keeping the outdated, dilapidated store, but another part reminded her this was her inheritance, her birthright. Back in Boston, she wanted to continue her education, and there were so many more demonstrations to march in for women's rights, events that focused on the plight of the American woman. And from what she'd seen in this small hokey town, women needed help here just like they did in Boston.

"We all assumed you would be returning to Boston," the man said, looking perplexed.

"I am."

"Then I thought you would want to sell the store," the

gentleman said.

Releasing a deep sigh, she stared at the man in a western suit and bolero tie. "I'm in no hurry to make any decision until I feel certain I've chosen the correct path. I've got time to make my decision."

The man nodded. "Returning after so many years of being separated from your father only to have him die must have given you a terrible case of the vapors. Please, miss, just remember I'm interested before you sell it to anyone else."

Abigail felt the hair on the back of her neck rise like a rabid dog. "I don't suffer from the vapors. I'm quite in control of my emotions regarding my father's business. I'll keep your offer in mind."

"Thank you," he said and walked away shaking his head.

The audacity of the man to try to buy her business before her father was even cold in the grave. Did the man have no shame? Couldn't the living at least wait until the dead were buried before they acted on their greed?

"Miss Vanderhooten," a tall gentleman said, taking her by the elbow and leading her into a corner where she pulled her arm away from him. He smiled. "I'm Tom Slate. Could I call upon you one day this week and take you to dinner?"

"I'm sorry, but I'll be in mourning for my father. I'm not accepting callers for a while."

He frowned. "Oh, yes. Well, when you're ready, I live here in the area, and I'm searching for a wife. I'd be more than obliged if you were to consider me as a candidate for your hand in marriage."

Of all the rude attempts by a man to garner her favors, this one scraped the icing off the cake and licked the knife. How dare this man approach her at her father's funeral?

"This is highly inappropriate. My father's not even been in the ground for a day, and you're wanting me to consider marriage?" she said, her voice rising in irritation. "No, sir. I'm not interested in wedding any man I don't have affections for."

The man looked chagrined. "Sorry, miss. There are just so few available women that when one comes along, a man has to do his best to beat out the other men. I wasn't going to let the grass grow before I requested your hand. And I would do whatever you require to garner your affections."

"Well, you could at least honor the memory of my father and wait until after the luncheon."

"Yes, miss," the man said and slinked away.

It was then that she felt a prickle along the back of her neck. She turned and saw Jack Turner standing in the corner watching her. A smile graced his face, and she had to resist the urge to swipe that smirk off his handsome features.

Oh my, today she'd buried her father, her last remaining parent, and so far she'd received one proposal and one offer to purchase the mercantile. And now this fool.

He strode over to her, his strong cheekbones and nose graced the well-defined bone structure of his face. His hazel eyes twinkled with a shining light, like he had a secret. "Miss Vanderhooten, my deepest sympathies with regards to your father."

"Thank you," she said, feeling like there was a 'but' in there.

"I hear you just received your first proposal."

"Of all the audacity of that man."

Jack threw back his head and laughed. "Please don't judge the men in our small town too harshly. There's a shortage of women, and when a young, beautiful, available lady like you comes to town, they don't remain single for long. And your father's business makes a woman like you doubly enticing."

There was something about this man that attracted and repelled her at the same time. One second she wanted to kiss him, and the next, she wanted to kick him in the shin. At her father's luncheon, she would try to act like the lady he expected of her.

She smiled. "Well, maybe the men in this town need to realize that pouncing on a woman before she's had time to adjust to the death of her father is a good way to find themselves blacklisted from the lady's favors."

"Agreed," he said. "But morals and values are a lot more relaxed out in the West than they are in Boston."

She stared at him. His sandy blond hair had streaks of gold that shone brightly. A wicked gleam sparkled from his eyes as they danced with merriment, like he could see she really wanted to kick him in the shin.

"When do you plan on returning to Boston?" he asked.

"I've not decided. I just arrived, and well, there are my father's affairs to consider, and even though I lived in Boston for many years, this is my home."

Right now, she just wanted to get through today. Today, she'd lost the last person on this earth who cared about her. She was alone, and that weight felt like an anchor around her heart.

She stared around the room. "So tell me, how many single men are living in this town that are young and vibrant and ready to marry?"

He shrugged. "Oh, probably close to thirty on any given day. I'm sure you'll receive more than one marriage proposal in the next few days."

"I'm not interested," she said. "You can tell your buddies I have no wish to marry anytime soon. How many businesses are in the town of New Hope?"

"Oh, about ten and when you close down your father's store, we'll be down to nine."

She smoothed her skirt. Close the store? At this

moment, all options were open. She didn't know what she intended to do, other than get this day behind her. "Who said I was planning on closing the store? How else am I going to earn a living?"

He hawed around for a moment. "Well, you do know the town of New Hope has an ordinance that states women can't own businesses?"

Abigail felt the air in her lungs tighten and freeze. She tilted her head and gazed at Mr. Turner. "What?" she said, shock coursing through her veins like a fine wine. "I mean why would the town care I'm now owner of my father's mercantile?"

She knew women were often at a disadvantage when they owned a business, but she'd never heard of there being a law against it.

Jack Turner nodded his head, his eyes widening. "The men who started the town thought women were to be seen and not heard. Their religion believed that a woman was to follow behind a man and focus on her husband and children."

Abigail laughed. "And just when was this town founded? Right after the pilgrims landed? It can't be that old."

"Our charter is dated 1836," he said softly. "The original settlers had to fight the Indians for our little piece of land. They wanted our town to follow the laws of their religion."

She shook her head. "Hang fire it's 1883. Don't you think that's archaic, even for a small frontier town?"

He shrugged. "I'm just the mayor. I make certain the rules are followed."

Jack was the *mayor*. She'd made those comments regarding the saloon, and he was the mayor.

"Did you take care of that noise problem?" she asked.

"I also own the saloon, and yes, the piano is no longer

being played quite so loudly, Miss Vanderhooten."

Oh my goodness, the man not only was the mayor, but he owned the saloon, the one whose piano you could hear half a mile from town. "Thank you."

The man was impossible, but what about the town's ordinance that no woman could own a business. Why did she feel like she should challenge this prejudiced law?

Abigail could feel her mind flying with this knowledge. Hadn't her sorority sisters and she just talked in jail about changing the world? Building their own town? Maybe New Hope needed Abigail and her sisterhood of friends. Maybe the men in this town needed to know women were just as capable at business as they were.

And maybe, just maybe, Abigail was the person who could stand them on end and make them pay attention.

"Why did you want to know the number of single men?" Jack asked, gazing at her like he could see the wheels of her mind turning and churning away.

She shrugged and smiled. "Let's just say I like law-abiding men just like every other woman, but I don't necessarily need to live in a town with such an archaic law. That just might have to change."

"Don't count on it."

Chapter Two

Three weeks later, Abigail ran a rag along the bare wood of the shelves, while Don sat behind the counter, reading the newspaper. Little by little, she was tackling the store, changing its appearance by rearranging and cleaning years of dust and neglect, while Don caught up on the news.

The bell over the door tinkled as a customer walked in.

Don looked up from his newspaper. "Good morning, Mrs. Smith. What can I do to help you?"

"I brought in a list of supplies I need. Could you please fill it and put it on my account?"

"Sure," he said, laying down his newspaper with a frown, not at all pleased to have been interrupted. Wasn't this his job? Wasn't Abigail paying him a salary to clean, stock, and deal with customers, and yet, he acted put out every time a client walked in the door and his reading was interrupted.

They'd already had one discussion about him purchasing the store from her. She feared if she sold the business her father and mother had created, Don would ruin their years of labor. So far, Abigail had been unable to relinquish her last remaining tie to her family. Quickly, she was coming to the realization she didn't know if she'd ever be able to let the business go.

Her roots, her family ties, and her legacy were here in this store. And right now, it just didn't feel right to sell her birthright. If she'd been a man, no one would be questioning her right to own this store, but because she was female they wanted her to sell.

Well, too bad.

The bell tinkled again, as the door opened. In walked her best friend, Bella, looking like the heat had all but melted her. Abigail ran to the front of the store, her heart pounding, tears gathering in the corners of her eyes.

"Abigail," her friend said weakly.

"Bella," she said, reaching out and throwing her arms around her. "My oh my, how I've missed you."

"Me too. I had to come see you," she said, gripping Abigail's hands tightly. "Is it always this warm here?"

Abigail laughed. "In the summer, yes." She gazed at her friend, her fellow demonstrator, her sorority sister and was overwhelmed with happiness. Since the day her father had died, she'd felt so alone. Such gut-wrenching aloneness that should have sent her packing for Boston, but instead, she seemed to be clinging to the past.

"How's your father?"

Abigail felt the sorrow reach out and grip her heart with a spasm that made her whole chest ache. "He died three weeks ago. My letter must not have reached Boston yet."

"I'm so sorry, sweetie."

Abigail nodded, unable to speak, knowing if she said anything, she would break down and cry.

"Well now, I'm even happier I came to visit. It was the right decision."

Nodding, Abigail hugged her tightly. "I'm so glad to see you. It was so kind of you to come. Follow me upstairs, and we'll get you settled in."

"Thank you," Bella said.

"Don, I'll be back down soon. Please take care of the store."

"Will do," he said in a sarcastic tone, picking up his paper once again after obviously watching the two women.

"He doesn't like me telling him what to do," Abigail whispered to Bella.

The two women giggled as they ascended the stairs at the back of the store.

In the living room, they settled into two facing armchairs. "Since my father died, I've been doing a lot of thinking about all of you and the National Women's Suffrage Association. How's it going?"

Besides her friends, being part of the women's movement in Boston was all she really missed. The winters were deplorable there, but attending college was fascinating and challenging and part of her longed to return.

"Everyone sends you their love. After you left, we all disobeyed the police captain and marched through town several more times. Last I knew, no one had been arrested, though the police continue to threaten us. We all miss you something terrible."

Bella's dark hair and earthy brown eyes stared at Abigail worriedly. "Are you okay?"

She nodded. "I'm trying to make some decisions about what to do with the store, my life. Whether I should return to Boston or stay here."

"You've got a lot on your mind," Bella said, glancing away. "And I came at the worst possible time."

"Oh no," Abigail said. "Actually, I'm so happy to see you. I didn't know what to do. Maybe you can help me."

Bella gazed at her. "How?"

"Do you remember when we were in jail and we were talking about creating our own town?" Abigail said, glancing at her friend, noticing the tired circles under her eyes.

"Yes, I thought it was just the boredom talking, but I remember."

"Since my papa died, I've been told that in this small town, a woman cannot own a business."

Bella sat straight up. "What? So how is she supposed to earn a living if she has no husband?"

Abigail smiled at her friend's reaction. Why was it that young women understood the vulnerability of being dependent on a man? Why couldn't men realize women just wanted the chance to have the same opportunities, the same chances in life they had?

"Oh, believe me, I've already received three proposals of marriage. The last one came in a handwritten note in flowers."

Bella started laughing. "You're kidding me."

Shaking her head, Abigail laughed as she told Bella about her latest proposal of marriage. "No, I never saw the man's face. I was to meet him at the church if I was ready to get married. He might still be down there, waiting for me to show up."

Giggling, Bella covered her mouth with her hand, her body shaking with mirth. "You're in mourning. You can't get married now."

"Doesn't matter. These men are desperate to find themselves a wife."

"I'm not that anxious that I'd marry just anyone," Bella said. "If I wanted a husband, I could have gone home."

Bella's family lived in St. Louis, where her father ran a shipping company on the mighty Mississippi river. Wealthy, she had never experienced a small town like New Hope. Abigail, wondered how Bella would like living without the arts and refinements of a larger city.

"Originally, I had plans to return to the university."

"You're no longer going?"

Abigail sat and considered the idea of returning to Boston. "I never thought I would say this, but I'm having a hard time letting go of the mercantile, which I've now received four offers on."

Bella started laughing again. "Is it men or women who want to buy the store?"

"Women are not allowed to own a business. We are to focus on our husband and children and let the men folk take care of us."

In a fairytale, it sounded so beautiful. A woman married

the man of her dreams, they had children, and while he worked to support them, she took care of his home and the children. But how many times had reality been different than the simple tale of love? And if a man was killed or, was a drunk or a heathen, how did the woman and her children survive then? How could she support them without the help of family and the generosity of friends?

"Again, what happens when something befalls that man or woman?"

Abigail shrugged her shoulders. "I don't know, but I think I'm about to test this law."

Bella giggled. "Yes, I can see you doing this."

"I feel the urge to show this town you cannot keep women down. I think we should contact our friends and tell them we have found the perfect place for women to take control of the businesses in this town."

"I love it," Bella said, leaning back in her chair. "Please warn them warm clothes are not needed before they get on the stage. I thought I would melt between here and Fort Worth."

Abigail smiled dreamily. "Each woman could have her own business. If she chooses to marry, there are lots of single men here. She could have both a business and a family."

"And a really good life, if she chooses her lifelong partner carefully."

"Only if she loves him. Marriage without love would be impossible."

"Yes, if you've already received three marriage proposals, I think these men are just looking for a woman, any woman. Someone to cook and clean and conceive a baby with," Bella said, shaking her head. "Is it wrong to reject the idea that a good husband is someone who comes with a large investment portfolio?"

For a moment Abigail wondered if Bella's father had

found her husband. He'd been threatening to for the last year, thinking his money for college could better be spent on a marriage or a merger, as he liked to call it. Surely, Bella would tell Abigail if that was the reason she was here.

"I think New Hope is about to get just that—a new influx of women with brains and a desire to control their destiny."

Abigail gazed at her friend so happy to see her. "So, you think it's a good idea?"

Bella smiled and shook her head. "Oh, Abigail, you have a way of finding trouble, squeezing every drop of life from it and then serving it at your next luncheon. I think it's a splendid idea."

Abigail reached out and grabbed Bella's hand. "I'm so glad you're here."

"How do you think the women in this town are going to respond?" Bella asked.

Abigail thought about the women who had set up the luncheon after her father's funeral. They were strong, caring women who held the community together. She would hate to receive their condemnation, but they needed to realize they were just as capable as men of owning a business.

"I don't know, Bella. That's my only concern because the men in this town need shaking up and thrown into the frying pan."

Abigail couldn't help but think of Jack Turner. His laughing smile, the way his hazel eyes twinkled, and the way he'd made a mockery of her by not helping her down and letting her think she needed to contact the mayor.

He was about to be in for the fight of his mayoral life.

"Nothing like tackling women's rights in the West."

~

Jack hated being thrust into this controversy, especially when the woman causing the problem was the luscious Miss Vanderhooten. Since the day he'd agreed to pick her up at the stage, he'd avoided her. The cool miss had gotten under his skin like stinging nettle.

But he had toned down the piano player in his saloon. When she'd pointed out the noise factor, he'd been shocked. He hadn't considered how much racket traveled down the street. Just because the woman had been right about the sound coming out of his saloon didn't mean he wanted to negotiate with her for her father's business. The law in New Hope said no woman could own a business, and as mayor it was his duty to carry out said law.

He opened the door and stepped into the mercantile. The store was empty, except for a young woman he'd never seen before standing behind the counter.

"Can I help you?" she asked.

"I'm looking for Miss Vanderhooten," he said, glancing around at the changes in the store. It looked cleaner, brighter, and more appealing. The displays were pretty and clever, tempting you to peruse the store a little longer. What had she done?

"Just a minute," the girl said, disappearing behind a wall. A few seconds later, she came back with Abigail, looking red-faced and wiping her hands on a rag.

"Jack," she said, "to what do I owe the pleasure of your visit?"

"Where's Don?" he asked.

"He's no longer employed here," Abigail said. "We had a parting of the ways."

He shook his head. So the rumors he was hearing were true. Abigail was putting herself in place to run the store against the wishes of the city council. "Do you have some place we can talk privately?"

"Jack, let me introduce you to my friend Bella

Spencer," she said.

"Nice to meet you, Mr. Turner."

"As well. I really think what we need to discuss should be in private."

"I have nothing to hide from Bella. She's my best friend."

Just what he didn't need, to have this discussion in front of another woman, a woman who'd come from Boston. He cleared his throat. "I've received another offer on the store. The buyer wanted me to present the offer to you to consider. He's willing to offer you top dollar for the business."

Abigail smiled at him, and he got the feeling she wasn't going to listen to him no matter what he said. He could just see the trouble seeming to ooze from her every pore, especially around her mouth. The urge to kiss those full lips into submission was overwhelming, and he blocked the thought from his mind.

The woman was a nuisance, and he suddenly wished she would just get back on the stage and ride out of town because there was something about her that was as tempting as crème filled rolls.

"I'm not interested in selling. This is my birthright. My father left me the store to do with as I will."

He took a deep breath. This was not going to be easy. "May I call you Abigail?"

"Of course, we're getting to be such good friends." She said the words with just enough sarcasm he knew he needed to be aware.

"You know the town of New Hope has an ordinance that no woman may own a business."

"Ridiculous," Bella said with a wave of her hand. "Complete nonsense."

Abigail smiled at him and lifted her chin defiantly. "So, what should I do? I don't want to sell."

"Then maybe you should marry, and the business will remain in your husband's name." The words made him cringe inside. Abigail marrying would be such a disappointment. Yet, that would keep him safe.

"But I'm not interested in marriage either," she said with a shrug and a complete lack of interest that piqued him.

A woman not interested in binding herself to a man…unusual.

He frowned. What kind of woman wasn't interested in getting married and having kids? Every woman he'd ever met wanted a man to take care of her. Now, he would be forced to give her the official mayoral speech.

"I didn't write the laws. But as mayor it's my job to make certain they're followed. You will need to either sell or get married and put the business in your husband's name."

"And if I don't? What are you going to do? Throw me in jail?" she asked with that saucy tilt to her head, her sapphire blue eyes just daring him to even try.

"If I have to."

She stepped around the counter and came to within inches of him. "Let me just say I will obtain a lawyer, and I will take this archaic law to the highest court in the land if needed. Does the city have the funds to fight a legal battle that will cost them a lot of money?"

He frowned as a trickle of annoyance spiraled down his spine. The city operated on a very tight budget with no room for extra expenses. Plus, next year he was up for reelection. How he handled this little problem could put all the wrong people in power. Not something he needed for this city that he cared about. "I will go back to the city council and tell them you intend to fight this ordinance."

She smiled. "Thank you, Jack. Tell them it's time they updated their laws to the nineteenth century."

He shook his head. "You scare me, Abigail Vanderhooten. Don't be surprised if you get backlash from the men in this community. Are you prepared for the men to take exception to your brazenness?"

"As mayor, it will be your job to make certain the sheriff protects me and my property from any men who may decide to partake in vigilante justice. As for my brazenness, you haven't seen anything yet, Mayor."

He stepped even closer to her and stared into her blue eyes. "Some things are out of my control."

"That's all I'm asking," she said.

"Nice to meet you, Mayor," Bella said as he turned and walked out the door.

He'd done his best to let her know what she was up against, but the woman didn't want to listen. He'd been witness to how a small Texas town could deal out justice, and even though Miss Vanderhooten was only trying to earn a living, he feared some people would find it bold and disrespectful. He only hoped his sheriff would protect her from the vigilantes who seemed to live in every town.

~

"Tell me about everyone. How are they doing?" Abigail asked Bella that night as they ate dinner in the Fork and Spoon.

"Emma has gone off to medical school. Faith is enrolled in law school. Everyone but Haley is still attending the university," Bella said. "Her father forced her to come home. She's getting married in the fall."

"Oh, dear," Abigail said. "I'm so glad you came here."

Bella smiled, but she seemed nervous. "I felt like you were off on a grand adventure without me. I wanted to go too."

"Not hardly." Abigail took a bite of her food. "Remember that class we took on selling? Merchandising

101?" She'd never thought she would use the knowledge, but now she found herself remembering things the professor had said about how to increase sales.

"How could I forget? That professor accused us of taking the wrong classes. He said we should be taking cooking or even elementary education classes." Bella shook her head at her friend. "Even in education, the men want us to continue in our assigned roles."

Laughing, Abigail said, "Yes, he did. But remember after we'd been in the class for a while, he did a lecture on how to increase sales? What if we were to create a display and for a limited time everything on the display is on sale?"

"We should try it. Have the sales fallen off since your father died?"

"No, but I fear by not selling the store and fighting the city, they will. When people learn I intend to take this clear to the Supreme Court, they'll be upset by how much this battle will cost the city."

Bella shook her head. "Why are you fighting this so hard? Why not sell and go back to Boston?"

"For several reasons," Abigail said, leaning over the table. "With the mercantile, I have a steady income. If I sell the store, I'll have a short-term financial gain, but would it be enough to let me finish college? Or would I have to go to work somewhere? And then I look around the place my mother and father created and I have such a hard-time letting go. This is my birthright. My inheritance."

A smile formed on Bella's lips. "And you're just itching to fight for your womanly rights."

Abigail couldn't suppress the grin that spread on her face as she shook her head. "This is going to be tougher than marching in Boston."

Just then, Ella Fletcher, the head of the ladies sewing group, walked up to their table. "Abigail, I wanted to stop by and offer my condolences on the death of your father."

"Thank you," Abigail said. "We were apart for so many years that I keep looking for his weekly letter. It feels like we're still apart, and he'll be sending me a letter any day now."

The woman patted Abigail on the back and then leaned down close. "I also wanted to tell you that if the rumors I'm hearing about you refusing to sell the mercantile are true, good for you. Many women in town have long believed that ridiculous law should have been overturned years ago. We're hoping you can get that straight for the ladies here."

"Thank you, Mrs. Fletcher. I appreciate your support and hope the men in New Hope won't run me out of business."

The older woman nodded. "I understand, but you keep fighting."

"Thank you, that means a lot to me."

Mrs. Fletcher walked out of the restaurant, and Abigail turned to Bella. "Maybe I do have support in this town after all."

"Or maybe she's just the random oddball," Bella said.

The cook appeared at their table and set down two pieces of fresh apple pie. "Compliments of me. Thanks for helping to get rid of that silly law. Even though I run the restaurant and do most of the cooking, we have to have the business in my brother's name because I'm a woman. And he gets part of the profit, but does none of the work. I'm sick of it."

"I'm so sorry," Abigail said, while Bella made a tsking noise. "Maybe what comes from it will help you as well."

"I hope so. Enjoy, ladies. I have to get back in the kitchen and finish cooking."

"Thanks, Henrietta," Abigail said.

"See, we can bring our cause out here to the West," Bella said. "Even here we can help change the world and make it a better place for women."

"I hope so, but I don't get the feeling the men will be as welcoming to change. After all, there are many of them who are looking for women and will see this as competition."

Bella shook her head. "You're wrong. Because they're desperate for a woman, a wife, a helpmate and partner, they're going to be open to accepting whatever the woman wants just so they have a companion. Actually, we may have a better chance of success right here in the West."

Abigail gave a little laugh. "This is why we're friends. You always help me see things in a different way. Thanks, Bella. Now let's just hope sales at the store will continue to climb as we fight this battle."

~

"What in the hell do you mean she's not going to sell? She has to," Tim Barton, one of Jack's city council members, yelled. "It's the law."

Jack stared at the men around the table. Returning here after attending college, he'd loved the town of New Hope, but some days he wondered why he'd ever gotten himself into politics and city government. It could drain the life right out of you, worse than any bullet hole he'd ever seen.

"I know, Tim, but the woman is threatening to take this fight to the highest court in the land. Do you know how much that will cost the city?" he said. "I estimated it, and we'll have to double the taxes on every citizen who lives here."

"She's just mouthing off. No decent judge is going to change this law."

"Send the sheriff over there and shut her down," Rupert Jackson said, an older man who had been on the city council for way too many years.

"Our nearest store would be in Mineral Wells. Are you ready to make weekly trips twenty miles away to buy what you need? How do you think the women in this town are going to feel about us shutting down a young woman trying to make a living and having to make a day's drive just to purchase supplies?"

Samuel O'Brien shook his head. "The women's opinions don't matter. They will obey their husbands."

Silence filled the room. Bernard Whitehouse laughed out loud. "Gentlemen, don't fool yourselves. Women have a way of getting even. They will make our lives miserable if we put this burden on them."

"Maybe you just need to lay the law down to your wife," Tim said. His great-grandfather was the one who'd put this ordinance on the books.

Another older man, George Potter—someone Jack had always listened to because his counsel was more prudent than the others—spoke up. "The world is changing. On the East Coast, women are marching in the streets for more rights."

"Hell, they can vote in Wyoming," Samuel said.

Tim shook his head. "No decent, God-fearing woman would want equal rights. She is to obey her husband."

Jack could see this conversation was quickly deteriorating. "Back to the problem at hand. Do we shut down the mercantile and prepare for a fight or let things continue on as is?"

Silence filled the room, and then George, the man with a logical brain said, "Let's invite the other business owners in town to the next city council meeting. Let's discuss this with them and see what their take is on the situation. We could boycott her, but once again, we'd have no store."

"Or someone else in town could open up a store and run her out of business."

Jack knew he would do whatever his council voted on, but part of him thought it was an archaic law. What did it matter? Shouldn't women be allowed to own a business?

The men started talking amongst themselves as to who had the most money and could open a competitive store.

Rupert pounded the gavel. "Excuse me, gentlemen. Before we approach the next city council meeting, what if we sent Jack to talk to her one more time? We tell her, here are your choices. One sell the store, two get married and put the store in your husband's name, or three take the city's law on and find yourself facing competition. Your choice. Then we finalize our decision when we meet again."

The men around the table nodded their heads, all except Tim. And Jack knew he wouldn't be happy until he'd closed Abigail down.

"Most women when faced with a problem of this magnitude will just sell the store. Personally, I think she's holding out for more money. No woman has the skill or the aptitude to run a mercantile," Samuel said smugly.

"Make a motion and we'll vote on it," Jack said, thinking that none of them knew Abigail like he did. The woman was intelligent and witty and more frustrating than a group of drunks on Saturday night, but he didn't doubt for a moment she intended to continue operating the mercantile. "I just want to go on record and say Abigail Vanderhooten is a very smart woman and considers that store her birthright. I don't think for a moment she's afraid of us."

The table grew silent, except for a pencil being tapped against the wooden top. Then William Fitzgerald made the motion Jack knew would stir up more trouble than a family of skunks.

Once the council meeting was over and the decision had been made, Jack walked back to his bar. He glanced around at the business.

"Mrs. Fletcher came looking for you. She's needing more of her arthritis medicine you give her," one of his bartenders said. "She'll be back later today."

"Thanks," Jack said. He'd gone to college with the intention of becoming a doctor, and instead, he'd become a pharmacist without a place to practice. After his father passed away and left him the saloon, Jack had added a small pharmacy in the back. So far, he only sold the drugs and prescriptions over the counter of the bar, but someday, he hoped to open his own pharmaceutical shop.

"How was the city council meeting?" his bartender asked.

"The next time I let you talk me into running for mayor, I think I will pull out a gun and shoot you."

"Well, you didn't want Tim Barton to take over the town, did you? We'd be shuttered before the ink was dry on the election results. That man is a religious zealot who thinks alcohol is the drink of the devil. He scares me."

"Well, he's still sitting on the council, and we're open."

"That's only because he hasn't gained control."

"Maybe so," Jack said with a sigh, knowing he needed to talk to Abigail and bring her up-to-date before someone on the council let their plans be known. He dreaded this conversation; though, he didn't mind gazing at the lovely young woman. She was a cute little pistol he feared would soon go off on him.

~

Abigail glanced up when the bell over the door tinkled, announcing the arrival of a customer. Jack strolled in, and her heart gave a few extra thumps. She couldn't deny the man was a looker, one every woman in town probably drooled over. She had to lick her lips to keep the spittle from appearing.

Why did the man have the ability to make her notice the way his shirt clung to his muscled chest and his pants fit snug against his thighs? Why did his big hazel eyes twinkle like they held a surprise?

"Good morning, Abigail," he said, walking up to the counter.

"Why do I get the feeling this isn't a shopping trip, but more of a social call?"

He grinned. "I'm officially here on city business."

"Oh," she said, gazing at him, wishing she didn't feel this attraction, knowing it could only get in the way. "Is this my official 'shut me down' visit?"

"The city council and I met yesterday. Here is the resolution we came up with for you to retain your father's store: one sell the store, two get married and put the store in your husband's name, three take the city's law on and find yourself facing competition."

Abigail felt her blood begin a slow boil. So, they wanted a fight. Well, she would give them a battle they had never even imagined.

Her lips felt almost brittle, as her smile turned cold. "That doesn't sound like a resolution. That sounds like a threat. So, you guys aim to put me out of business if I don't comply with your outdated archaic law?"

A tense grin appeared on Jack's face. She could see him struggling. "Let's just say you will face competition."

Her stomach clenched at the realization they meant to run her out of business if she didn't concede. Well, think again. There would be letters going out to her women's sorority tomorrow, inviting them to come to New Hope and open up shops, especially because the small town needed the business. Somehow, she would find a way to bring this town's codes into the nineteenth century, where women held jobs and earned a living without the aid of a man.

"Are you giving me a date I need to comply by?" she asked.

A sheepish expression crossed his face. "I need to let them know at the next city council meeting, which will be held next week."

"Where do they meet?" she asked, wondering if she had time to gather a group of women to back her.

"This is a special meeting being held in the church," he said. "But you can't attend if that's what you're thinking."

"Why not? Their decision will affect my future. Why can't I tell them in person how I intend to handle this situation?"

Did they really think she would just take this sitting down? That she would give up her birthright just because some idiot law said only a man could own a business?

"Because frankly, I don't want to have to protect you from how these men will react with violence," he said, his voice low and deep, sending a shiver down her spine. Was that shiver a result of fear or the way the she could get lost in his gaze?

Never before had a man attracted her or affected her senses like this one. He was dangerous to both her independence and her libido, and she needed to put him off.

"I think the next time you come into *my* store you should buy something or not come in at all," she said, staring into those eyes she could get lost in. "This is a place of business."

He smiled. "I'll take two peppermint sticks, please."

She pulled them out of the candy box and handed them to him. "That will be a quarter."

"Candy has certainly gone up in price," he said, shaking his head.

"The price goes up when there's the threat of competition. I have to earn as much as I can before I'm run out of business. You must understand that feeling when the churches in town try to shut down the saloon."

There were women marching in towns across America trying to eradicate demon alcohol. All she wanted was the same rights and privileges men were afforded. She didn't care if they wanted to take a drink or two. She just wanted to earn a living, have access to a bank loan, own her own business, and vote.

He nodded. "Very much."

"You have a great day, Mayor," she said sarcastically, dismissing him. He was now the enemy. She would have to find a lawyer before next week and not one from the town of New Hope.

"You as well, Abigail." He turned and walked out the door, and anxiety assaulted Abigail.

What if she was run out of town or what if they brought in competition? She could lose the very thing she was trying so desperately to hang onto.

Bella came around the corner and stared at Abigail. "Sorry, I couldn't help but overhear. What are you going to do?"

"I'm going to send our friends an invitation to open up a trade in this wretched town. I'll tell them how the town has an ordinance that women cannot own a business and that if we have to, we'll move just outside the city limits and set up shop."

Wrapping her arms around her middle, Bella considered her. "I get the feeling the mayor is just as confused as you are right now. He didn't seem to really enjoy delivering this message. I think he might be a little sweet on you. And you, you're glowing like a bride."

"No, I'm not."

"Well, there certainly is a glow about you."

Abigail glared at her friend. "It's because I'm so mad I just want to march through town, shouting at the women to wake up."

With a laugh, Bella reached out and rubbed Abigail's arm. "I think you're going to need to wait on the others before you do something like that. It wouldn't take much to throw two troublemaking girls in jail. But a group…that could draw unwanted attention to this small town. Don't worry. We'll get this changed."

"You're right," Abigail said with a sigh. She knew from past experience nothing changed overnight. Sometimes it took years, but eventually New Hope would have to recognize women had rights just like men, just like they'd had to eventually give the blacks their rights. This was no longer a white man's society, but everyone's.

"Is there anything I can do for you?" Bella asked, glancing at Abigail worriedly.

"Yes, rid me of this attraction I feel for the mayor and help me write letters to our friends. It's time to bring this town into the nineteenth century."

Chapter Three

On the return walk to the saloon, Mrs. Whitehouse, one of the councilmen's wives, approached Jack. He tipped his hat in greeting and she stopped.

Laying her hand on his arm, she gazed up at him. "Mr. Turner, my husband has told me about the council's plans, and I'm on my way right now to purchase all of our groceries from Miss Vanderhooten. The young woman inherited her store, and what this town is doing is wrong."

Jack nodded. "Don't tell me. Explain it to the men on the council. I agree with you."

"I told my husband he's playing with dynamite if he thinks the women in this town are going to accept what the council is doing to Abigail. It's time the women in our fair city were treated with respect, and this law is outdated. I intend to talk to the sewing club about this egregious law. Hopefully, I can convince them to support Abigail."

She frowned at Jack like he was the culprit behind the council's behavior, and he knew Tim Barton would love how the women would blame him for the outcome of this situation if the council got their way. What would happen if they learned the council wanted to put in place competition to the young woman's store?

"Mrs. Whitehouse, I am doing what I can, but once the city council gets involved in running her out of town, then there's not much I can do."

She smiled. "I'm going to call upon each one of the city councilman's wives and just see about that. This is Walter Vanderhooten's daughter, he was a respected member of our community, and we should defer to his wishes. He left the business to his daughter. Now the city council should leave her alone."

Jack smiled and knew the Whitehouse home would not be a pleasant house tonight. "Yes, ma'am. I don't disagree, but I'm just the mayor, and it's my job to carry out the law."

Lucy Whitehouse looked up at him, her blue eyes filled with concern. "You're in a tough position, mayor. Maybe what should happen is for women to run for city council and take over this town?"

Wouldn't that put starch in Tim's drawers to learn the women were considering taking over the city council? But since they couldn't even vote in the city elections, they would be hard pressed to win.

Sometimes you just had to let the other person feel they had the power. "Women governing our small town would be a great addition, but once again, that's against the law," he said. "At least for now."

She shook her head. "I've got to run, but I wanted you to know not everyone in town is happy with the city council's decision."

"Thank you, Mrs. Whitehouse, for letting me know," he said and tipped his hat to her as he continued down the sidewalk.

He'd barely gone five steps when two other women halted him.

"Mayor, a word with you, please."

"Good morning, Mrs. Jackson and Mrs. Fitzgerald."

"Is it true?" Mrs. Jackson asked.

"What are you referring to?" he asked, knowing without her saying a word what she was going to say. They were going to make his life a living hell for the next week.

"Is it true the city council is going to shut down the mercantile?"

Jack took a deep breath and again recited his stand. "Our city has an ordinance in place that does not allow for women to own a business. You can put the business in your father's or your husband's name, but a woman cannot be the actual owner."

"That's outlandish. She inherited this business," Mrs. Fitzgerald said her hands on her hips. "Her father clearly wanted her to own the store."

"What's wrong with a woman owning a business? Sometimes we need to work just like a man does to feed our families. Sometimes life doesn't give us any choice but to take care of ourselves," Mrs. Jackson said, her voice strong with indignation.

Standing in the street as the wagons rolled by, Jack felt like people were frowning upon them as this woman gave him an ear full on why a woman needed to own a business.

"I understand, Mrs. Jackson. I agree with you, but the city ordinance makes it impossible for her to keep her inheritance," he said gently, knowing he was riling these women up with the word *inheritance*, hoping it would come back to haunt the city council. Knowing it would probably affect him as well. Tim would use this in next year's reelection campaign.

Jack really didn't care if she kept the business. Women were not a threat to him, and he certainly had no desire to own her mercantile.

"That's right. Her father owned that store, and he left it to her. No, the city council should not be able to take away her birthright. That's so wrong. Mrs. Jackson and I are on our way to our Bible study group. I'm going to tell the women there."

"If you feel strongly about this, you should attend the next city council meeting. That's where the final decision will be made to shut her down," Jack said, knowing if the place were packed with women, it would be hard for the council to ignore them.

Mrs. Jackson smiled. "Women love a good fight, and you're about to have one on your hands, Mayor."

He shrugged. "Don't blame me. I just carry out the council's orders here in our little town. I'm the tiebreaker vote. The other six individuals create the laws I oversee."

The woman puffed up her chest. "When is that meeting?"

"Next Wednesday at noon in the church."

"I can't wait to see you and the city council men, Mayor."

"Good day, ladies," Jack said as he tipped his hat and continued on down the street.

This kind of fight was not good for the town or families or men. One way or another, he needed to bring this to an end right away or watch a division created with the men on one side and the ladies on the other.

The two sexes battling each other was not good business for their small little village. In some way, he had to help resolve this conflict before it became an all-out war.

Maybe he should ask Abigail to dinner. Maybe over dinner they could have a logical discussion of why this fight needed to end.

Later that afternoon, he sent one of his employees to her with a handwritten note, extending a dinner invitation that evening at the Fork and Spoon café. In the note, he said to let him know if she could make it.

Thirty minutes later, he was doing inventory on the liquor when he heard the scrape of wood against wood, and the men in the bar sounded like they were almost choking. He turned around, and there was Abigail. She strolled into his saloon, wearing what he was certain was the latest fashion. The bodice of her dress fitted her upper torso, shaping her breasts and making her waist tiny. The skirt was pulled back and tucked into a bustle that moved when she walked. A parasol made her appear like a lady out for a stroll. The men all stood like soldiers at attention as she walked amongst them, heading for his bar.

The woman had nerve. His saloon was exclusively for men. No women allowed. She'd just broken one of the biggest taboos in town for a lady, and she acted like she really didn't care.

The woman had guts and was brazen, yet looked so soft and vulnerable. And goodness, that dress hugged all her curves and made her look good enough to want to slowly unwrap each layer to reveal the hidden prize.

When she reached the bar, she turned toward the men. "Thank you, you may be seated, gentlemen."

Crossing his arms, he gazed at her, wanting to bend her over his knee and paddle her, but knowing if he touched her, that wouldn't be good. Because he feared once he started, he wouldn't be able to stop. And a saloon was hardly the place to put his hands on the lady. "You are bound and determined to get thrown out of town, aren't you?"

"Whatever do you mean, Jack?" she asked all innocent and doe-eyed.

"Women are not allowed in saloons. City ordinance number twenty-five."

She raised her brows at him in a haughty manner. "America, land of the free. I can go just about anywhere I want to."

He shook his head and laughed. "Well, Miss Betsy Ross, let me escort you to the sidewalk."

"Afraid to talk to me in here?" she asked, turning to glance at all of the men sitting at tables, watching them.

"I'm the mayor. It looks really bad when I break the laws," he said, not wanting any of the city councilmen to walk by and see the gorgeous temptress in his saloon.

"They're stupid laws," she said.

"That may be so, but until they're rescinded, I am duty bound to obey them."

She stared at him with her eyes all big and blue and her mouth oh-so tempting. "Well, then get to it. Update that odious scroll of outdated decrees."

He shook his head. "You know I should make you buy something for coming into my place of business. After all, you made me buy something at yours."

"Recommend something to me, and I'll buy it."

Taking her by the elbow, he walked her back through the crowd of men to the door, not about to open the temptation to serve her liquor. When they went through the swinging doors, the silent bar suddenly erupted in laughter.

Abigail frowned. "Your men seem to think it's funny when a lady visits your den of inequity."

He shrugged. "You've given my customers some entertainment this afternoon. I should be thanking you for that."

"Glad I could be of service. Now, about this dinner invitation… What's the occasion?" she said, her eyes all wide and blue.

"No occasion. I just thought it would give us a chance to get to know one another a little more. I could give you the town's reasoning behind these archaic laws."

His hand felt right, gripping her elbow as they leaned against the outside wall of the saloon away from the swinging doors, but still under the awning. They were certainly drawing the interest of the people on the street as they passed.

"If this is going to be a night of you trying to convince me to sell the store, then we might as well end this conversation right now. I'm keeping my store, and I'm winning this battle," she said, her eyes flashing defiant.

He placed his fingers beneath her chin and tilted her head up, staring into those eyes that reminded him of bluebonnets in spring. A searing heat started in his groin, and he released her chin. "Now, Miss Vanderhooten, I wanted the honor of getting to know you better, to find out why you are so determined to hang on to that dilapidated store."

So, he was lying. Sure, he wanted to spend time with her, but he also was going to try to convince her to end this fight. People were taking sides. It could get ugly.

She smiled. "I'll meet you at the café at seven tonight. Bring your dictionary as you're going to be looking up a number of words that will explain why I'm keeping my posh new store."

He frowned. Had she done some remodeling? It would be too obvious to go by now and check it out. What if the changes she made catered to the women in this town? They were sorely missing a shop of their own since Mr. James had closed his women's boutique. If she catered to the women, they would stand behind her even more.

"See you then," she said, walking down the sidewalk away from his saloon.

Abigail was way too smart and business savvy; she knew exactly what she was doing if she had restocked her store for the female shopper.

~

Promptly at seven o'clock, Jack was standing outside the café, waiting for the luscious Miss Vanderhooten. He felt a tug on his jacket and turned around. There she was, standing behind him in a lovely green dress that fitted her curves. She carried a small purse, and a warm feeling filled him at the sight of her. Why had this woman awaken his long sleeping desire and had him thinking thoughts of just how she looked beneath that beautiful dress?

He halted his thoughts before he undressed her. He didn't need to imagine Abigail without her clothes on. He didn't need that kind of torture.

"Good evening," she said. "I took the long way, so I could get some exercise and clear my head. I've been working in the store, rearranging things all day and needed some fresh air."

He smiled down at her. She was such a petite little thing, but looks could be deceiving. Behind those beautiful blue eyes and gorgeous blonde hair was a mind that was way too smart for her own good, and she had a will of iron.

Rearranging? Yes, he'd bet his last dollar she was preparing her store for the female buyer. And if so, this could become an all-out war between the men and women.

"I'm starving. Let's go eat," he said, gazing at her, wishing they weren't on opposing sides and he was courting her, instead of plying her with food for information. But he hadn't courted a woman since college.

As they settled in at a table, she glanced around the room, taking in people's obvious interest in the couple. Several men waved to him and smiled knowingly.

"Well, aren't we the couple of the hour," she said, smiling at the people staring.

"It's because you're with the mayor," he said and winked at her, knowing the gossip would be flowing through town, worse than a spring flash flood and possibly as dangerous.

If the town had a newspaper, this would be headline news in the morning edition. By tomorrow afternoon, someone would have created a rumor they were courting, and they'd be married by sundown. All in the name of gossip.

"Maybe they're afraid I'm going to influence you, and by the time we're done, you'll be instructing the council to reform those outdated laws and let women own businesses," she said, her brows lifted, a smile on her full mouth.

Boy, how he would like to taste those saucy lips, run his fingers across them, and stroke her face. But that couldn't happen. That would certainly give the gossips something to tattle on about.

"I think I've already fallen under your spell. I'm going

to have to resign and let all you ladies take over," he said, laughing at her, wishing they were alone.

The cook came over, and they ordered their meals, and then they sat there looking at each other. How quickly could he get his purpose accomplished, and then get this beautiful woman escorted home, putting as much distance as possible between the two of them? She was not the type of woman he normally felt such an attraction to, and she was dangerous. The woman was nothing but trouble, the kind he didn't need.

"How's the store doing since your father died?" he asked.

She smiled. "I know you want me to sell, and you're probably trying to keep customers from coming in, but so far it's not working."

Part of him was relieved her business was still doing well. "I assure you I've done nothing to affect your business." He may not have done anything to stop the clients from coming in, but he knew the council members were instructing everyone they knew not to shop there.

"I've invited the women's sewing club to meet once a month in the back of the store. There they can discuss the latest fashions and how to create them. On that day, I'm giving them a ten percent discount on any sewing notions they purchase. We're in discussions now with another group of women to start a woman's auxiliary club, and we're offering the store as a meeting space."

The women of New Hope had never shown an interest in being involved in a civic way, and he could see Abigail was winning them over. Slowly, she would indoctrinate them into her politics. How would the city council handle a women's movement in their small town? Because he feared that was where this was headed.

"You're really catering to the women in this town," he said, worry rushing through him and settling in the pit of his stomach. The men would not want to see their women change.

"Yes, I am. I'm going to start holding one event a week that will have a women's group meeting there. I would love to include the men's groups, but right now I don't trust you guys to behave yourselves. Not when I receive at least one warning a day that I should sell."

He leaned forward in his chair. This was the first he'd heard that she was being threatened. That wouldn't do. "Are they threatening you personally?"

"Not so far, but just like today, a man came in and offered to buy the store from me. He told me I should seriously consider his offer before I ruined the value of the store." She shook her head. "After all, I don't have a brain in my pretty little head, and I'm just here for birthing babies and taking care of my man—if I can get a husband."

Jack threw back his head in laughter. The woman had a wicked sense of humor, and he had already heard this sentiment spoken more than once in town by men. Keep your woman under control in the home. Keep her pregnant.

"I didn't tell the man I was considered the smartest woman in my class at Boston University or that I was getting a business degree."

Jack gazed at her, admiring the way her blonde hair was piled in a chignon atop her head, and her sapphire eyes left him feeling warm. "So, why aren't you selling the store and going back to school?"

She sighed. "The money I make from the sale would probably get me through my degree. But then, to continue on, I would be forced to marry a man to live comfortably or take a job I'd hate. I don't want to get married. If I married, my business would automatically be put in my husband's name. I'd lose total control. I like being in charge of my destiny, of having choices."

"How many marriage proposals have you received?" he

asked, knowing there was a group of men who were constantly searching for a woman. Some had even resorted to mail order brides.

"At least one a day," she said with a laugh. "One of the first ones sent me a note and told me to meet him at the court house, and we could take care of getting married right away. I'd never even met the man."

Jack felt a surge of anger at the unknown man. Yet, he knew the men in this area wanted the business. She came as part of what they wanted, and they'd accept her as part of the deal, as long as they made all the decisions.

"You have to understand our town was founded by a religious group of settlers. The men believed women have no say. You are to bear children and cook and clean for the family. That's your sole purpose in life."

Abigail smiled. "Hogwash. I'm a human being. I have just as much right as a man."

He laughed. "I'm not saying I believe that, but I'm trying to give you the history of the town. Most women want to get married and have children. Why don't you?" he asked, wondering what this school she'd attended had taught her.

"I want to get married, but I intend to marry for love," she said.

Love? What a naïve notion. "It doesn't work that way. People get married for companionship and to have a family," he replied, shaking his head at her sadly. "And most of the time, the father chooses the woman's husband."

"Well, my father is dead. I have no uncles. So, who is going to choose for me? That's an outdated system. If I don't love the man, then I'm not going to marry him. I don't need him."

He glanced around the diner. "Do you think everyone in this restaurant loves each other?"

She furrowed her brow at him. "Absolutely not. How

many women in this restaurant, if given the chance, would leave their husbands today?"

"We're not talking marriage; we're talking business. Look around. These marriages are businesses. Marriage based businesses. That's what these women are—they needed to be taken care of. The man offered and was accepted. It's not about love," he said shaking his head.

She smiled. "My point exactly. For most of these women, their husband was chosen for them. Some of the marriages turned out happy; some did not. If they had property when they married, it went to their husband. I'm not going to live my life that way. I want a man who is my companion, my lover, my business partner, not my owner, my boss or my master. I can't live that way."

"That's a naïve school girl's attitude. That's not realistic or possible," he said, thinking about his own parent's marriage and how miserable they were together. What he'd seen was the reason he had no intention of ever marrying.

She smiled. "Most people think so, but I'm an educated, modern young woman, and I don't intend to live like my ancestors did. It's time for women to change the world, and I plan on being a part of that change."

He just about spewed his food. "And how do you intend to do that?"

"I'm a member of the National Women's Suffrage Association. I marched in Boston with women for change. Over time, I intend to bring that movement here."

"Oh no, you're not," he said louder than he intended.

She smiled. "You can't stop me."

"If you keep this up, you're going to be an old maid."

Busting into laughing, she shook her head. "That's a scary threat. Living without a man."

The woman was making fun of him. She was laughing at the idea of never marrying. He'd never met anyone like her. She intrigued him, made him want to know her better.

She tilted her beautiful head at him, and all he could think about was taking her in his arms and kissing that smart, full mouth of hers. Of nibbling on her saucy lips until she went limp in his arms. That could never happen because he could never act on this attraction he felt toward this sprite of a woman.

"What does it matter? If I don't find the right man, I'll be an old maid anyway," she said with a defiant tilt to her head.

"That kind of love is only real in fairy tales. It does not exist in real life."

She shook her head at him. "No, Mr. Turner, it does. It's very real, and I hope you find it someday."

He glanced down at his food. The woman was wishing his idea of hell on him, and yet, he couldn't help but want to spend more time with her. "You are going to make my life difficult, aren't you?"

"Whatever are you talking about? How will I make your life difficult?"

"I'm supposed to convince you to give up your fight, sell your store, and get out of town, but I don't think I'm getting anywhere."

She laughed, the sound a soft melody that sent tingles down his spine. He couldn't remember the last woman who had affected him this way. But, this couldn't happen. She was the wrong woman in the right place at the wrong time. *No, no, no.*

"Not a chance. I'm not selling, and I'm not leaving. I'm going to bring my friends here to help settle the town with modern young women doing business."

He glanced up from his food and stared at her. Fear radiated through him at the idea of what this would do to their small community. "No, you can't do that."

"Why not? Some of my fellow NWSA sisters are on

their way here now."

"Dear God, you wouldn't," he said under his breath.

She smiled. "Already done. The first woman should arrive in two weeks."

Jack stared at the beautiful woman in front of him. He was in so much trouble. New Hope would never be the same after the women from Boston arrived. How would the city council take this news? And did he dare tell them, or should he let them find out on their own, the hard way?

~

On their way out of the café, Jack reached for Abigail's hand and placed it in the crook of his arm.

She glanced up at him, her brows raised. Why was he being so polite?

"Excuse me, but my mother raised me to always be well mannered to a lady, and therefore, I will escort you back to the mercantile," he said.

"Don't let me harm your male sensibilities," she said. "I enjoy being treated like a lady."

To her amazement, Abigail had enjoyed her dinner with the handsome mayor. She hadn't planned on taking pleasure with him, but he was actually fun and entertaining. The evening had flown by, and when the restaurant had started closing, they'd had their final battle over who was paying the bill. When he'd announced that his manhood would forever be damaged by her paying the tab, she'd relented. Lord help her, she didn't ever want to permanently scar the poor man, but she already had plans on how she could get even.

"Thank goodness for that," he said. "I was beginning to wonder."

"I just want to have the same rights and privileges as a man. I want to be treated as an equal."

Why was it so hard for a man to understand that a

woman wanted to be treated like a lady, but not as if her brain cells were only capable of cooking and reproducing. There was so much more between her ears that insisted on experiencing everything life had to offer.

"But you're the weaker sex. Men are supposed to take care of women and children," he said. "That's our purpose on earth."

"And that's a great manly attitude, but I'm just as smart as a man. And I need to know how to take care of myself, in case a man is not around or if I just want to be an equal. There's room here for us to work together." Without endangering a man's pride.

Oh rubbish, men seemed threatened by the very idea of a woman learning as much as she could about life and participating in it.

"Lord, I pity your poor husband…if you ever find a man willing to put up with your beliefs."

"My mentor in Boston was married. They were happy and very much in love."

In the darkness, she could see him shaking his head. "The man was certainly no cowboy, and I bet he was soft."

"Mr. Minor was a college weightlifter, a businessman, and a professor at the college."

"Oh, he was one of those scholarly types. All books."

"He was a weightlifter."

"Honey, I lift weights every day when I pick up a barrel of whiskey. Weightlifting is not impressive. Most men do it all the time," Jack said, patting her arm and gazing down at her.

She laughed. "Adam was tall and skinny, but Elizabeth loved him with all her heart, and they seemed happy. That's more than I can say about most people."

Their shoes made a clomping noise as they walked along the wooden sidewalk headed toward the mercantile, away from the restaurant and the saloon. The evening breeze blew cool for the first time that day, and Abigail knew in the coming months even after the sun went down the breeze would still be hot. But for now, she was enjoying the night air.

"Most couples appear happy in public; it's the scenes behind closed doors that expose the truth."

That was revealing. It sounded like he knew from personal experience and had witnessed an unhappy couple. Could it have been his family?

She didn't know anything about his clan. All night long he'd never said a word that would divulge his background.

Just then, they arrived at the front door of the store. She wanted to invite him in and ask him about his kin, but she knew that wouldn't be proper, and her reputation was already notorious. She didn't need to add insult to injury.

She turned to face him. "Tonight was the best time I've had since I arrived in New Hope. Thank you for such an entertaining evening."

Nodding, he moved closer to her. "You certainly keep things lively. I couldn't believe Henrietta had to run us out of the restaurant. I had a good time."

A bug landed on her cheek, and he swiped it away, touching her skin in the process. Heat shimmered through her, and she stared up at him in surprise. "I should go in. The skitters are getting bad."

"It's late," he said breathlessly, his eyes gazing at her with what appeared to be longing. The longing she'd been fighting all night long. They were enemies. They were on opposite sides of the cause, yet she'd enjoyed being with him tonight.

He leaned down and his mouth touched hers gently. Shock filtered through her, but it was a pleasant surprise, and she slanted toward him, her hands reaching out and grasping his arms to hold on. His lips moved over hers, his tongue caressing her, and she opened up to him. He pulled her into his body, and she could feel the hard muscles beneath his shirt. She'd been kissed before, but never like this, never like he wanted to consume her, to eat her up in the process. A raging heat built in her center like a slow fire. Nothing like she'd ever felt with any man.

Then suddenly he released her mouth. She opened her eyes slowly to find his big hazel eyes gazing into hers.

He smiled. "You are trouble."

She released him.

He stepped back and tipped his hat to her. "Good night, Abigail."

"Good night, Jack. I'm a good kind of trouble."

She could hear him laughing as he walked down the street. What had she just done? She'd kissed the mayor, and she'd liked the feel of his lips on hers. She liked the mayor.

~

The next day, Jack was not surprised when two of the city council members showed up in his saloon, the worst two city councilmen.

"Jack, heard you had dinner with Miss Vanderhooten last night. Any luck on convincing her to sell that store?"

Jack leaned across the bar. "Hello, gentlemen, good day to you. Are you interested in having a drink?"

"Thank you, but I don't drink, Jack," Samuel O'Brien said, glancing around uneasily in the saloon. "The women in this town are gathering behind Miss Vanderhooten. We don't need them all riled up because we're forcing her out of town."

Jack gazed at Tim Barton who stood with his arms crossed, frowning. Both of these council members would love to see someone other than Jack be mayor. In fact, he'd beaten Tim out of the position, and the man was eager for the next showdown.

"You should have already shut her down," Tim accused, glaring at Jack like he was a gunman. "Her father knew the law and should have found her a husband before he died."

"It's her livelihood. It's how she earns money to take care of herself. Her father was a respected member of this town, and I refuse to do anything to dishonor his memory. Not to mention our citizens buy their supplies from her mercantile."

If the women in this town heard Tim disrespecting Walter, they would be stringing him up by his toes. Walter Vanderhooten had been a friend to many women. A good listener, there to help with buying their supplies, he was not the person Tim should be badmouthing.

"It doesn't matter. It's against the law."

"Well, maybe she's right. It's an outdated law," Jack said, wishing this would all just go away. Everything, except Abigail. He'd enjoyed last night's kiss. He'd enjoyed that delectable mouth of hers and the way they had spared over dinner.

Sam's eyes widened. "You can't take her side."

They would love to pin this on him, so they could use it against him at reelection.

"I'm not. You're right. It's against our current law, but until I have made sure all other recourse has been pursued, I'm not shutting her down."

"You've got to do something," Tim said, stepping closer, a surly look on his face. "Our women are taking her side. My own wife is telling me we're being ridiculous to shut down the town's only store. I've forbidden her to shop at the mercantile, and she's told me I can drive the wagon over to the next town if I don't like her shopping there. In fact, I can do the shopping and the cooking as far as she's concerned."

Jack had to restrain the laugh he felt building up inside

him. This overbearing, egotistical, cold-hearted man had the sweetest wife. He'd wondered for years how the woman lived with the religious fanatic who treated his wife more like a slave than a lover.

"Yes, and MaryAnn told me if I helped shut the mercantile down, I could sleep out in the barn. We don't need this kind of rebellion from our women. They are to obey their husbands, take care of their families, and be God-fearing, church-going women," Sam said.

Part of Jack agreed the women should be God-fearing and church-going, but another part of him wondered how it had gotten this way. Weren't married couples supposed to work together rather than have the man hold control over the woman as if she were a child instead of an adult capable of making decisions?

"Now, don't be too quick to judge," he answered. "I believe Miss Vanderhooten has been in church each and every Sunday since she's been home. She even volunteered to visit the widow women, if you recall."

"Attending Sunday service and being a follower of our laws are two different things. She needs to sell that store, get married, or get out of town. And frankly, I'm just fine with her leaving town. I'll even buy her a one-way ticket on the next stage," Tim said, a smug smile on his face like he was being generous.

Oh, if he only knew the suffragettes were on their way to their fair city, the man would probably drop dead right there in Jack's saloon, and Jack didn't need the kind of attention that would cause.

"You've got the town dividing into factions, Mayor. It's the men against the women. We don't need that in our city, our businesses, and most of all not in our homes. Get rid of this girl or shut her down," Sam insisted.

These two would run her out of town tonight if they knew the other women like Abigail were arriving soon.

Come what may, he was going to have to protect Abigail, and he knew she wasn't going to like him watching out for her or even having the sheriff watch over her.

"Gentleman, you're going to have to settle down and give me a little more time. This will be settled at the city council meeting next week. Something will be decided by that time. So sit back, pacify your wives, and wait." And rest for the coming storm because like a hurricane, it was headed in their direction.

Tim shook his head. "I don't like waiting that long. You should have done something before now. But since you're mayor and I'm not, we'll do this your way. But reelection is coming up next year. And this is a clear case of lack of leadership on your part."

Until Tim Barton had decided to run for mayor, Jack had never considered city politics, but the man was cold and ruthless, and Jack was afraid of what Tim would have done to their fair city.

Jack smiled and leaned across the bar. "You do that, Tim. Just because I don't want to throw a young woman out in the street and sell her birthright, doesn't mean I lack leadership. It means I have a heart, which I'm fairly certain you're missing. I will see you gentlemen at the city council meeting, unless you'd like to buy a drink, and then I'm more than happy to pour you a whiskey."

Just then, the piano player started banging the keys on the piano. The music was loud enough it ended the conversation. Jack needed to give that man a raise.

Tim started to say something when Sam pushed him toward the exit. Jack couldn't help but wish the swinging doors would slap both of them in the rear end as they left.

Chapter Four

Abigail had not been able to stop thinking about that kiss all day. She'd found herself working in the store, humming, and then she'd stop and touch her lips and wonder what had made his kiss so different? She hadn't wanted him to stop caressing her. In fact, she'd wanted him to continue.

Why Jack Turner? What about him made her think about the way his mouth moved across her own, the probing of his tongue, and the way he'd held her tight against him? She liked his smile, the way he laughed, and how he seemed smart. Smarter than she'd expected for a bartender. Yet, he was still determined to shut her down, and that could never happen.

They were on opposite sides, and she would do well to remember that, regardless of the way he made her feel.

She walked outside and glanced down the sidewalk. When her father built the mercantile, he'd made the building large enough that he could either expand the store or he could rent out sections to other shop owners. Right now, there three empty sections with her store in the middle.

This morning she'd awoken to the fact that none of the other women would be able to rent places in town when they arrived. Yet, she had the capability of renting to at least three of the women, maybe more.

Staring down the street, she saw the saloon where Jack tended bar. With her purse in hand, she strolled toward his business, eager to confront the handsome man. She waved to several women she knew from church. When she reached Jack's saloon, she could hear the music spilling out the doors. It was just past two in the afternoon, and she didn't think it would be very busy, but she had to show him he couldn't get the upper hand. Though last night he'd certainly made progress, she was here to take back the power.

She twisted her reticule in her hands then pushed through the swinging doors. With her shoulders squared, her head held high, and her bonnet strings tied tightly beneath her chin, she walked into the saloon like she belonged here.

The music screeched to a halt as all the men stared at her in amazement. She'd entered the men's forbidden territory once again.

Jack swore and shook his head. "What are you doing? You know this is against the law."

"I've come to pay you a visit," she said grinning, getting just the kind of reaction she wanted from him. Feeling like a rose in the desert, she noticed the glances she was receiving were not exactly welcoming.

"You're not supposed to be in here," he said.

She shrugged and took a seat on a stool at the bar, showing him she was here to stay. "It's another one of those archaic laws that needs to change. I'd like to order a drink please."

"Are you old enough?" he teased.

"Of course," she said.

"What if we don't serve alcohol to women?"

"Then I'm not leaving until I get a drink. I would think you would want me to get out of here quickly."

He laughed. "If we don't allow women in here, then we certainly don't sell them a drink."

"Are you going to get me a drink or not?" she asked. She wanted to demonstrate to him how out of date these types of laws were. If a woman wanted a drink, she should be able to get one.

"I'm breaking the city ordinance serving you."

"I don't care."

With a shrug, he said, "Okay, what is it you want?"

Other than drinking a little sherry, she had no idea what hard alcohol tasted like. "I don't know. What's good?"

"Oh, there are a lot of liquors that are good. But the key is knowing what you want."

"What do most men order?"

"Whiskey," he said.

"I'll take one, please."

"You don't want to do this," he said shaking his head, his hazel eyes twinkling with amusement.

An uncomfortable feeling of being out of place had assailed her the moment she sank onto the bar stool, but she ignored the persistent warning. "If a man can drink it, so can a woman."

"Okay," he said. "But I'm warning you. You're not going to like the liquor."

"Just pour the drink." She watched as he pulled a bottle off the shelves and splashed the alcohol into the glass then slid it over to her. "Thank you, how much do I owe you?"

"This one's on the house."

"No. I wanted to buy it to repay you for dinner last night. You bought candy in my store and my dinner. It's the least I can do."

"Dinner was on me. The drink is on the saloon."

She sighed. "Okay, but after this one, I'll take another one, and I want to buy it, so I've helped your business, so we're even."

"Just get through the first one," he said laughing.

She knew what he was thinking. He didn't think she could get the first one down. Picking up the glass, she brought it to her lips, and the smell just about knocked her off the stool. Doubts about what she was doing assailed her. She glanced up at Jack. "How do you drink this?"

He poured himself a glass. He lifted his snifter and clinked it against hers. "Bottoms up."

She watched him drink the liquor in one gulp.

"That's how."

"Oh, my," she said. "I thought you would sip it."

"Not whiskey."

Picking up the snifter, she put it to her lips and drank it one big gulp. Fire spread through her mouth to her lungs and her chest and she gasped. She couldn't breathe. Tears welled up in her eyes and she coughed.

Jack ran around the counter and patted her on the back. "Why do you think you have to do everything a man does? Some things are better left alone."

She straightened her back and glared at him. Once she could breathe again, she wanted to slap that smart comment right back into his brain, but she would do even better. She took a deep breath. "Give me another drink."

"No."

"Mr. Turner, I am a paying customer." She dug the money out of her reticule and slapped it down on the counter. "Another whiskey."

He sighed. "All right, but in a moment you're going to start feeling the effects of the alcohol. You're a novice, and one drink would have probably made you feel woozy, but two drinks are going to make you soft as butter."

Interesting theory, but still she was not going to let the man win one over on her. She would prevail and come out ahead. "That's no concern of yours. I'm quite capable of walking back to my store."

"Sure you are," he said in that sarcastic tone she was beginning to recognize.

She watched him pour her another drink, gazing at his lips and wondering if he would kiss her again. That had felt good. Really good. Tilting her head, she questioned if he had some magical trick he did when he kissed a woman. The smooches she'd experienced in college had been dull. In fact, most of them had been downright gross. Just a slobbering mashing of two mouths so that most of the time she'd wanted to wipe the back of her hand across her lips to clear the taste. But Jack's were different, much different and much better.

She picked up the glass and gulped the liquor. This time the burn was slower, and in fact, delicious warmth spread through her chest. She licked her lips and set the empty back on the counter. "You know if I was to drink a couple more of those, they wouldn't be half bad."

"Oh no, you've had enough for a beginner. I think it's time for me to walk you back to the store because very soon you're going to feel the effects of that liquor, and you're going to regret those drinks."

Frowning at him, she wondered why the hurry? She was enjoying his company. "Why don't you show me your business? I'd like to see how it operates."

He picked up the two glasses and put them away. "You are always so curious. Maybe some other time when you can remember what I show you."

"I'll remember it now," she said, her lips not wanting to work properly. She touched her fingers to her mouth. They felt numb. What had she done?

"Tell me that in about ten minutes. Come on, let's get you home," he said, walking around the counter and taking her by the arm.

Sliding off the bar stool, she stood and arranged her dress, then smiled at him. When she took the first step, her legs felt a little wobbly. Like her knees were turning to mush and would soon collapse. "Oh, my."

Glancing at her, he frowned. "You okay?"

She grinned at him. There was no need to worry the poor man, and she would soon be back at the mercantile. "Of course, I am. Let's go."

The first few steps were good. She marched through the saloon. "Goodbye, gentlemen. Maybe I'll come back and have another drink soon."

They all frowned at her. Why were men so grumpy all the time? Didn't they know women were fun? Didn't they enjoy the company and attention of a woman?

She ran smack dab into the door. A giggle rose up inside her, and she bent over laughing. "Oh, my."

"Are you okay?" Jack asked.

She straightened. "I'm perfectly fine. Your door is off kilter. Look, it's hanging crooked."

"Sure, you're fine," he said and she felt him take her by the arm.

They stepped out into the sunshine. "Tell me something, Mr. Turner. Why did you kiss me last night?"

"Because I wanted to."

"Why did you want to?"

"You ask a hell of a lot of questions, lady," he said with a tight grip on her arm.

"I want answers. What did you do to my lips? I've never been kissed like that before. It felt good, real good."

He laughed. "I kissed you passionately. Whoever you've been kissing must not have known how to do it properly."

She could feel the frown drawing her forehead together. "I've only been kissed twice in my life. Once by Smithy Jones and another time by Matthew Pender. Both were dreadful bores."

"Good day, Mayor," a woman called.

"Good day," Abigail responded, smiling and waving.

"You might want to just walk beside me quietly," Jack said, "so as not to draw too much attention to the fact you've over imbibed. I think the two of us out together is drawing enough attention without showing everyone you're drunk."

"I did not over imbibe. A lady does not drink too much hard liquor."

"I'm not going to question if you're lady."

"I am a lady."

"Well, if you're not drunk, then I should let you walk back to the store alone," he said, letting go of her arm.

Abigail felt as if her feet were walking on board the deck of a ship that was rising and falling on a wave in the sea. "Whoa, why is the sidewalk moving?"

He laughed and grabbed her arm again. "Yes, you're drunk."

"It's not a bad feeling."

No wonder men liked to hang out at the bar and drink until they could no longer walk. The alcohol made you feel warm and calm and relaxed.

"Not yet it isn't, but just wait. Either this evening or tomorrow morning, you're going to wish you'd never heard of demon alcohol."

"This is not a demon. More like a warm blanket."

Jack laughed out loud at her. The man was beginning to irritate her with his smart comments and making fun of her.

They arrived at the mercantile. "Who's watching the store?"

"My friend Bella. She's the first one of my friends to arrive. You're going to love them all. They are such great women. Strong and independent, fighting for equality."

He shook his head. "Good Lord, I better get you inside before you start preaching women's rights, right here on the sidewalk."

She turned and looked up at him. "Preaching? I'm merely telling you about these wonderful women who are going to change the world. They'll go down in history."

"Yes, and my grandfather was General Lee."

She stopped. "Really?"

"No. Now come on, we better get inside the store. I just hope for once you don't have any customers." Opening the door, he helped her into the building.

"Bella, I'm back," she called.

The young woman came around the corner and stopped. "Oh, my God. You're drunk."

Abigail laughed. "Yes, I am. I had two drinks of whiskey at Mr. Turner's saloon. They weren't bad. I mean the first one just about killed me, but the second one went down nice and smooth and left such a pleasant warm feeling."

"Maybe we better get you upstairs and let you lie down and rest."

"Okay," Abigail said with a giggle. She turned to Jack. "Thank you for the drinks. I really enjoyed them. And thanks for the kiss last night."

He smiled at her. "You're welcome, but I'm concerned with you walking up those stairs. Are you certain you can make it?"

"Bella will help me. Good day, Jack Turner." She waved to him.

"Good day, Abigail."

Abigail wrapped her arm around Bella's waist. "He's not bad. In fact, he's kind of nice."

When they got to the third step, they stumbled. Jack was right there to catch them. Without his help, they would have fallen to the ground.

Abigail giggled. "I don't think I can climb the stairs."

"Let me help you," he said and swung her up into his arms.

She clasped her hands behind his head, and he hurried up the stairs. "Wow, you are so strong. This is how I've always envisioned my husband taking me up to bed the first time."

Jack stared down at her, and she could feel the heat from his gaze even in her dazed state, but he didn't respond to her admission about her wedding night.

"Which room is yours?" he asked gruffly.

"The one on the right," she said.

He turned into the bedroom and set her down on the floor.

"Will you kiss me again?"

For a moment, he hesitated. Then his mouth covered hers. The feel of lips was even better this time. This time she felt like her knees were going to collapse as he sapped the strength from her body, and she wanted more. So much more.

Abruptly, he let go of her mouth.

When she opened her eyes, he was staring down at her. "Where did you learn to kiss like that?"

He laughed. "That's my secret."

"Wow, if you could bottle that up, I could sell a million of them."

"I need to be going."

She grabbed his shirt and pulled him to her one more time. She kissed him this time.

He stepped out of the kiss. "Good day, Abigail. You might want to take some aspirin later today to help with the headache."

"Good day, Jack," she said, rubbing her hand across her mouth. "Next time we're going to talk about our businesses," she said with a hiccup.

~

Abigail's head throbbed like the beat of a drum. Poor Bella had been stuck running the store yesterday afternoon and taken care of Abigail last night. Her stomach had refused the taste of whiskey, and she'd lost her lunch. Then this morning she'd awoken with her head pounding, lethargic, and crankier than a mama bear.

Whatever the ingredients in whiskey were, they weren't agreeable, and she regretted trying to show him she was just as capable as the next man of holding her drink. She couldn't and wouldn't ever try again.

"A Mrs. Barton is here to see you," Bella said.

Abigail ever so slowly and gently went downstairs. Whatever the woman wanted, Abigail hoped it was quick, so she could lie down again. Only when she was flat did her head not pound out the rhythm of her heart.

"Abigail, are you feeling okay? I was quite concerned when I heard you'd gone into the saloon," Mrs. Emily Barton said, gazing over Abigail like she could see the alcohol oozing from Abigail's pores.

"I'm fine. Just a little under the weather today."

"Can we sit and chat?"

"Sure, come back here to the parlor," Abigail said, leading the way. "Would you like some tea?"

"Oh no, I won't be long."

They sank into the posh chairs Abigail's mother had upholstered.

Emily glanced around the room, looking uncomfortable. "First off, I wanted to come by today and let you know the women in town are with you in recalling this horrible law. Yes, my husband is one of the council members, but just about every woman in town I've spoken with wanted me to tell you to continue the fight. Personally, I've refused to cook for my husband and I told him I wasn't going to drive twenty miles to another store. So therefore, he can go without eating."

Abigail smiled. Part of her felt excited the women were standing up for her, but another part knew this would only make the men angrier. This could be the reason nothing had been done yet. Every day she expected to wake up and find out she'd been shut down.

"Thank you. I appreciate your support so much," she said. "It means the world to me."

"But, Abigail, when you go into a saloon and drink the men's liquor, that gives our husbands even more reason to want you gone. They're watching you. You've got to be on your best behavior, or you'll lose to the men," the woman said gently. "I don't think you understood what you were doing yesterday, or at least, I hope not."

She was correct. Abigail had made a huge mistake going to the saloon. She knew better, but the ever-powerful attraction to Jack had her seeking him out and wanting to get even for buying her dinner. She'd even asked him why his kisses were so powerful and begged him to do it again.

"You're right. Jack bought me dinner the night before, and I wanted to pay him back by purchasing a glass of whiskey. Only I'd never had alcohol before. I won't do that again."

The woman sighed. "Good. We want you to win your fight with the city. It's time someone stood up for the women in this town." She rose from her seat. "I've got to go before Tim finds out I'm here. He'd be most upset."

Abigail walked her to the door. "Thanks for coming to talk to me, Emily. I'm so glad the women are behind me, and I promise there won't be any more trips to the saloon."

"Great," Emily said and gave Abigail a quick hug. "Good luck with your fight. Be strong."

"Thank you," Abigail said and shut the door behind her.

Turning around, she faced Bella. "The women in this town are waking up. They're with us."

~

Later that same day, the bell above the door tinkled and Abigail came out from the back with a greeting. "Hello."

Two angry looking men walked up to the counter.

"Miss Abigail Vanderhooten?"

"That's me," she said, a trickle of fear scurrying down her spine.

"I'm Tim Barton from the city council, and this is Sam O'Brien from the council. You're breaking the law by owning this business." The man's face was an ugly twist, and for a moment, Abigail feared he was going to crawl over the counter and threaten her.

She took a step back. "My father has been dead less than a month, and you expect me to have the mercantile sold?" she asked, trying to stall the inevitable.

"There are any number of buyers wanting to purchase this place, and you've refused every one of them."

How did a sweet woman like Emily put up with a brute of a man like this? She had been so nice and sincere, and this man was like a raging bull. The only thing missing was the drool coming from his mouth, and Abigail expected that at any moment.

"This is my birthright. My father left it to me in his will. The business is mine," she said softly. Her determination caused her to raise her chin and meet his gaze head on.

The man slammed his fist down on the counter. "I don't care. We are here to uphold the law, and there's an ordinance in this town that says a woman cannot own a business or property. That includes your birthright."

Abigail felt the bristles rise on the back of her neck. The man was crazy.

She smiled at him. "Don't you think that law has been on the books a little too long? That maybe it's time for it to go away?"

The man's face turned red, and she feared he would drop dead from anger right there in her store. That would certainly not be good for business.

"No, I do not. My faith tells me women are to be seen and not heard. You have no power, and you cannot own anything," Sam O'Brien said, standing by Tim.

"My faith tells me God would want me to be able to take care of myself and to help others in the process. Currently, I employ my good friend Bella, but I'm hoping soon I will be able to hire more women to help me run the store."

Tim shook his head. "No. This needs to stop now. By the end of next week, you'll be shut down if not sooner. I'd highly suggest you sell this business and get out of town. We don't need your kind living here, influencing our women. We only want women who are Godly and obey their husbands."

She laughed. "You don't need a wife. You need a child who has to ask papa for permission. I feel sorry for Emily. A man who takes care of his wife and treats her as an equal, that's a real man."

The man's eyes darkened with anger, and she saw his fists clench at his side. Fear raced along her spine, causing her knees to quiver.

"Get out of town, Miss Vanderhooten, before it's too late, before the wrath of the town council runs you out of town."

Anger at the man's abuse roared through her like a lion, and her fear disappeared. She doubled up her fists and leaned over the counter. "Listen here, I'm not going to let you or anyone else scare me into selling. I'm not leaving the store my father built. I'm not leaving my birthright. Now, I think it's time you gentlemen left before I contact the newspaper and tell them I'm being harassed by the city government."

Chapter Five

Jack pulled his wagon up in front of the store. He had worried all day yesterday about Abigail, but he hadn't had a chance to check on her. Plus, he was afraid she'd throw something at him if she felt as bad as he imagined.

Alcohol sickness was something he gave up years ago. His limit was one drink on Saturday night to celebrate the end of his workweek. The rest of the time he stayed away from liquor. When you served it every day, you saw the unpleasant effects on people.

After stepping down from the wagon, he tied the horses to the hitching post then opened the door to the mercantile. His breath stopped at the sight of Abigail bent over, her skirts falling to the front, exposing the back of her legs almost to her knees. The woman had nice legs that went with the rest of that luscious body she kept under tight wraps.

She jumped up and blew the hair away from her mouth. Her face was red, her blonde hair disheveled, and her mouth so full and ripe and tempting. She looked good enough to eat.

"Good afternoon," he said. "How are you feeling?"

She frowned at him and shook her head. "You should be ashamed of yourself for selling that poison."

He laughed and walked the rest of the way into the store. "I didn't force you to drink it. In fact, I warned you, and you insisted on a second glass."

She put down the rag in her hands and approached him. "Today, I feel better. But yesterday, I would have thanked anyone who shot me and put me out of my misery."

The urge to reach out and stroke her soft skin was almost unbearable. She was so cute, all messy looking with her attitude firmly back in place. The woman he enjoyed was certainly in fine form. "Anytime you feel like you want to try whiskey again, let me know."

Shaking her head, she said, "I received a visit from Emily Barton warning me about the dangers of going into the saloon. Proper ladies did not go into that evil place. Then later that afternoon, I had a visit from your fellow city councilmen. Did you send them calling on me?"

He frowned. This was a direct disobedience of the instructions he'd given the council. "I've told everyone we are to wait and make a decision at next week's meeting. I've sent no one to speak with you. Who visited you?" Without her saying so, he knew it had to have been the jackass and his cohort in crime. Those two could stir up more crap in town than a gossipy group of women. They were worse than any ladies auxiliary he'd ever dealt with, including that bunch who wanted to outlaw liquor.

"Tim Barton and Samuel O'Brien," she said quietly. "They warned me to get out of town."

His stomach clenched as rage roared through his body like a wild herd of horses out on the plains. Before the day was over, he'd speak to the sheriff about keeping an eye on Abigail and her store. Sometimes men lost their heads over the silliest causes, especially when they felt endangered. And Tim's ego was as fragile as china on a shelf in a hurricane.

"This afternoon, I'm driving out to check on some property I'm considering buying. Would you like to ride along?" he asked. He hadn't intended to ask her to go with him, but just seeing her caused him to long to spend more time with the spirited little blonde.

She glanced around the store. Her friend came to the door that separated the living quarters from the retail area of the building. "I can watch the store this afternoon. In fact, I just fixed some lunch. Why don't you two take it and have a picnic? If you'll give me five minutes, I can have it all wrapped up for you."

"Bella, that's okay. You don't have to do that," Abigail said, walking toward her friend.

"After yesterday, you could use the outing. Now, just give me a moment to get this all together."

"If you don't mind," Abigail said, pulling down the rest of her hair. All those blonde curls spilled around her shoulders, and he suddenly ached with longing to touch it.

She ran her fingers through it, and in a matter of seconds had it pinned back up off her neck. She removed her apron and grabbed her reticule off the counter.

A picnic sounded great. The weather was perfect, the sky was clear, and the wildflowers were just starting to fade. It would be an ideal day to have an outing.

"I'm all set. I just hope the ladies from church don't mind me going chaperonless with the bar owner."

He smiled. "Seems to me if anything inappropriate was going to happen, it could have been when you came into my saloon."

Bella came back through the door with a basket. "I put in some fried chicken, canned fruit, napkins, and a jar of water. You two enjoy."

Taking Abigail by the elbow, Jack led her toward the door. She turned and waved goodbye to Bella.

Once outside, Jack helped Abigail into the wagon, untied the horses, and climbed in beside her. He clicked to the team to get them moving.

People stopped and stared at him riding out of town with Abigail.

"Oh no, the gossips are going to be busy this afternoon."

"I don't care," he said. "We're not going to be gone long. If anyone asks, I'll tell them we were looking at property out of town for you to build your new store on."

She laughed. "That would solve my problem, wouldn't it?"

"Yes, it would." But she wouldn't be close enough for him to keep an eye on her, and that thought didn't exactly sit well with him. The simplest thing would be to refute the law and end this fight.

Stunned, he realized he really did want her to stay, and he wanted her to retain the rights to her store. He was leaning against his city council and more toward Abigail, and that could hurt him.

"No one could tell me I'm breaking any laws."

"Nope. But you'd be more endangered for break-ins and robbery." He didn't like the idea of her being where he couldn't get to her. Especially with idiots like Tim Barton so fearful she would lead the women against him.

They rode along in silence for a few moments before she asked, "Where are we going?"

"I'm looking at some property along the river that's come up for sale. I've been considering moving my living quarters out of town."

"Why?"

"Well, I get tired of living above the saloon. It's noisy and smoky. I guess I make a lousy saloon owner. It's not something I enjoy doing." If the saloon had not belonged to his father and put Jack through college, he probably would have sold it years ago. His brother had long ago walked away from the business, saying he wanted nothing to do with taking care of drunks. And Jack couldn't blame him. After all, there were nights Jack felt the only ones who came into the place were the men who couldn't make it another hour without liquor.

"You went to college. Why aren't you doing what you love?" she asked.

He shrugged. "The saloon was my father's, and I just hate to part with it. But I don't enjoy the work."

They rode several more minutes before he finally pulled the buggy to a halt. "Here it is."

The land had splashes of bright yellow wildflowers with fading bluebonnets and Indian paints. The flowers waved in the wind like water ebbing and flowing. Big gnarled oak trees covered a section of the property, and in the back, he could see the Brazos River meandering like a lazy old man.

He ground tethered the horses and then came around to help Abigail out of the wagon. He wrapped his hands around her tiny waist and lifted her to the ground. Just the act of touching her had his heart banging inside his chest like the bell from the church.

She placed both of her hands on his chest, and when her feet touched the ground, she smiled at him in a way that sent his blood racing.

Without thinking, he leaned down and covered her lips with his. She moved into his arms, wrapping her hands around his neck, as he explored her mouth. The woman fit perfectly beneath his chin, snug against his body, her breasts pressed against his chest, her center in the perfect spot.

Suddenly, she stepped out of his arms, her breathing fast and shallow, and her eyes wide with wonder. "Those lips of yours are dangerous. They make a girl forget herself."

He laughed and lifted the picnic basket out of the wagon. "I've never been told that before, but it certainly does feed my ego. Glad to hear it."

"Of course it would. But then again, you men are so easy," she said with a laugh.

They walked up the small knoll to the top of the land, where they could see the river, and he placed a blanket beneath an oak tree. She sank to the ground and unloaded the basket. He dropped down beside her.

"Bella is a great cook, so I know this chicken will be good."

"What kind of cook are you?" he asked.

"The worst," she said. "I think the food I fix is boring. For some women cooking comes natural, but not for me. What about you?"

"I can cook. I took a lot of chemistry in college, and I think that helped my cooking skills."

"So why aren't you doing what you love full-time?" she asked, handing him a plate loaded with chicken and bread.

He shrugged. "The saloon put me through college. My father was a rough man, but he wanted his children to be educated. He only went to school through the sixth grade and insisted I attend college. But he wanted me to become either a banker or a businessman. While taking a science class one day, I fell in love with chemistry. Eventually, I narrowed it down to pharmaceuticals. The doctor tells the patient what kind of drugs they need, and I prepare the dosage for them."

While he'd been attending college, the field of medicine and pharmaceuticals seemed to explode with knowledge. Some of his professors had been physicians in the Civil War, and their knowledge of preparing medicines while out in the field was extraordinary.

"You're almost a doctor," she said, gazing at him like he was the smartest man.

In their small town, few people recognized his knowledge. After all, he was just the saloonkeeper's son. Her praise made him feel ten feet tall.

"I thought about studying medicine, but creating tonics and pills and cough medicine was so much more interesting. Now instead of owning a drug store, I hand out pills from the back of the saloon."

"That must be difficult. Running a business you don't love."

"Yes, it's a compromise. I'm doing what I enjoy, but I'm still working the saloon."

They ate their cold fried chicken with slices of homemade bread. Later, he opened the canned peaches, and they took turns eating the sliced fruit straight out of the jar. When they finished, she put everything back into the basket.

"That was really good. Be sure to tell Bella thank you," he said, lying back on the blanket, thinking how pleasant it was out here with Abigail. There were no worries, no pressure, and they'd not even discussed the upcoming decision regarding her store. It was just the two of them. There was something about this woman he really enjoyed.

She lay back on the blanket and gazed up at the sky with him. "Look, that cloud is an angel with wings."

"How did you get that? I thought it looked like an Indian with a bow and arrow."

She laughed. "And that one over there is a birthday cake."

"Okay, I'll agree with you on that one." He rolled over closer to her, so wanting to pull her into his arms, but he didn't want to seem too forward. Still, just the idea of her lying next to or on top of him was enough to have his manhood standing at attention.

"Why have you never married?"

The food in his stomach seemed to swell as he tensed. He didn't like talking about his family. Not everyone had a happy home life. Yet, he couldn't explain his views on marriage without telling her about his parents.

"In college, I was determined to get my education to please my father. Afterwards, he died the first year I was home. I honestly believe he was just waiting for me to get home from school."

"Do you know how unusual it is for a man from a small western town to have attended college?"

"Yes. Do you know how unusual it is for a woman from a small western town to have attended college?"

She sighed. "I wanted to finish school."

Abigail's father had been a good man. What she didn't know was how long he'd been ill and had kept the knowledge from her, letting her stay as long as possible in Boston. He hadn't sent for his daughter until he knew his time on this earth was almost over. Jack had admired the man. He'd always been fair and honest in his dealings with the people in town.

"That doesn't answer my question about why you've never married."

Like a miner, the woman was determined to unearth his reason.

"If you notice, there are not a lot of single women in our town. And most men don't want their daughters marrying the saloon owner."

She rolled over and faced him, her head resting on her hand as she half sat up, her shimmering blue eyes warm and soft. "There are other options. You could have gotten a mail-order bride. You could have gone to another town."

He shrugged and sighed. "My parents' marriage was not a happy one. Remember the other night when you said something about the women in the café, how many would leave if they could? That would have been my mother. Your words perfectly described her life."

A frown graced Abigail's beautiful face, and he could see she was concerned.

"Oh, I didn't know."

"It's okay. My parents didn't love one another. Before she died, she told me the only reason she married my father was to get away from her parents. She needed some place to go, and he was the only option."

Abigail closed her eyes and shook her head for a moment. "That shouldn't be a woman's only choice. She should have been able to take care of herself, made a living, and then if she wanted to, gotten married."

"What am I going to do with you?" he asked, gazing at her, knowing he was so attracted to her. He wanted to pull her down on the blanket right now and crawl over her and have his way with this luscious beauty. But that would be wrong.

"Keep me in town, running my store," she said gazing at him quizzically.

"Did you send for the other women to come?"

"Yes, and all of them are single. The town should soon be filled with women who want to marry and have children and own businesses."

He chuckled. "You're going to keep me busy as mayor, aren't you?"

"If you keep that archaic law around, yeah, your life is going to be interesting."

Jack stared at her and rubbed his fingers along her cheekbone. Her skin was so soft and tempting. He pulled her head down to his mouth, where his lips plundered hers once again. This woman had the ability to rattle him clear to his bones. She was soft and tender on the inside and tough as nails on the outside, and he understood why. His own mother had been a victimized woman and been forced to accept a man she didn't love as her husband.

Abigail only wanted the ability to take care of herself. He liked her strong, stubborn attitude.

He pulled back from the kiss and gazed into her dreamy eyes. "You know this is going to get us both into trouble."

"Yes," she said breathlessly. "Especially if you vote to close me down. I can promise you I will never speak to you again."

Rubbing his hand through his hair, he wanted to promise her that would never happen, but he knew he couldn't. "I'm the mayor, Abigail. I have to obey the laws of the town. I may not have any choice."

"And I want to continue the store my father built and

devoted his life to."

How could he blame her? Wasn't that the same reason why he'd refused to sell the saloon? It wasn't that he enjoyed watching men fill themselves with liquor and stumble out the door. Sure, it provided him with a good living, but he would so much rather be creating tonics and medicines that would heal the town people, rather than doling out alcohol that would eventually rot their brains and stomachs.

"How about you? Why have you never married?"

"Never met a man I've fallen in love with. My mother died when I was really young, but from what few memories I have, I know my parents loved each other. And I know my dad still missed her after all these years."

"You were lucky," he said, remembering the atmosphere of his family home during his childhood. "Watching people fight day in and out makes you think of only one thing, escaping."

"Do you have any brothers or sisters?" she asked.

He grimaced. "Yes. I have one of each. My sister, she followed the pattern of my mother. She wanted out of the house and married a man she now hates. And my brother…my brother is married and has two kids. He seems genuinely happy. He even told me he loves his wife very much. I can see how my parents' relationship affected all of us. It's sad."

"But your brother is happy."

"Yes, but he hasn't convinced me love is the answer. I think he may have just gotten lucky and found a woman he's compatible with."

"No, I think your brother decided he wasn't going to let his past affect him. He chose happiness."

Jack stared at her, tossing her comment around in his head. "I'm not unhappy. I like my life. I just don't want to risk everything on a marriage that could turn out like my parents'."

She shook her head. "Not if you love the person you marry. That's what my parents had, and I won't settle for anything less."

What an inexperienced schoolgirl idea. Didn't she know love was not real?

Jack cared about his brother and sister. He wished them the very best and would do everything he could to help them, but he couldn't say he loved them. The closest person he could say he'd loved was his mother, and that was only because he'd wanted her to be proud of him. But no other woman had ever made him feel the tender emotion, if it was even real.

"But how do you know you're in love? I wouldn't have a clue what that emotion looks or feels like. It could walk up and slap me upside the head, and I'd just think I have a headache."

Plucking a piece of grass, she put the blade between her luscious lips and gazed at him. "My father told me it's when you can't stop thinking about the other person, and you want to make them happy. He said it's when you'll sacrifice your own happiness for theirs."

He carefully considered her words. The only example of love in his life was his mother's love for her children. Even though she hated his father, she had loved each one of them and told them over and over how great they were and how they made her proud. She'd sacrificed for them, and he'd loved her with all his heart.

"Me, I just need the perfect man, and I'll be ready to fall in love," she said, rolling back and staring up at the sky again

Jack sat up laughing. "Now, that's the response of a naïve girl. There are no perfect men and no perfect woman."

She sat up and glared at him. "I'm not naïve. And yes, I

know figuratively speaking there are no perfect men. But I want a man who can accept me for who I am. And I haven't met one yet who didn't have problems with my 'radical' ideas, as one suitor called them."

She stood and picked their picnic items off the blanket. "We need to get back. I don't want the women in town joining the men's side because they think I'm a loose woman."

He stood and helped her fold the blanket. "The men are worried. Their women are taking your side, and you're messing with their home life."

"I don't understand why it's such a big deal that I own my family business. Would they rather I take up prostitution in order to eat? It's just so ridiculous. Their wives would be in the same predicament if something happened to their husbands."

"The men see you as a threat. Their women are agreeing with you, and you want to change the way they've done business for the last thirty years in this town. You're the unknown, and they're afraid. The next thing you'll want is to vote."

She laughed. "You are so right. I want to own a business, property, be able to get a loan, and yes, I want to vote. Why shouldn't I have a say in who governs the city or country where I live? Maybe the war would never have happened if women had been in charge and didn't want to see their husbands and sons killed."

Jack shook his head. "Do me a favor. Don't ever say this to anyone else. Because if you do, I can guarantee you will never be allowed to stay in town. Let's just work on getting you the right to own your family business first. Then later, after things have calmed down, you can tackle those other issues. But the men in this town are already afraid, and you'll be run out of town if they learn what else you want."

She was looking at him strangely, her head tilted. "You just used the word 'let's' like you plan on helping me. Do you mean to help me?"

He took her in his arms. "Like I've said before, I'm the mayor, and I have to enforce the current laws. But yes, I think you should be allowed to own your family business."

She reached up and gave him a brief kiss on the lips. "Thank you."

Jack's chest swelled, and he knew he had to get her back to town or do something entirely disrespectful like spread that blanket out again and take her right there beneath the blue Texas sky. This woman was tearing him up inside, and he didn't know how to handle her. He'd never experienced this feeling before, and it frightened him.

~

When he pulled the wagon up in front of the mercantile, the sun was sinking into the western sky. The town was starting to close down for the night, and the saloon would soon begin its busiest time.

"I guess I better get to work," he said, helping her out of the wagon, "but I enjoyed the afternoon. Would you like to have dinner with me tomorrow night?"

She smiled at him. "Yes, but don't you think the townspeople are going to start talking about us?"

He laughed. "Honey, they've been talking about us since your father died." He watched as her eyes widened in disbelief. "And another thing, stay out of my bar."

"Well, that's not very inviting," she said in a snit.

"No, but I don't want to give the church ladies any more reason to talk about us and even possibly shut me down." In other cities, the women were doing their best to run the saloons out of town. He didn't need the aggravation. In his saloon, if you got drunk, you were escorted out the door.

"Oh," Abigail said, walking toward the store. She turned and glanced back at him. "You know when you tell me not to do something, that just makes me want to show you I can."

"Okay, I'm asking you politely not to show up in my saloon again."

"That's better. I'll take it under consideration."

He grinned at her, shook his head, and clicked to the horses. The woman was next to impossible, yet he had this insistent need to spend more time with her. She was intriguing, thought provoking, and he'd never met another woman like her before.

Chapter Six

Abigail walked into the store, shut the door behind her, and sighed. There were so many things about Jack Turner she liked. No man had ever sparred with her before, and she thoroughly enjoyed tangling with him.

And the man's kisses had her thinking thoughts no decent woman was supposed to have, yet her body seemed to gravitate toward him. When he kissed her, she wanted to rip her clothes off and let him have his way with her, and no man had ever interested her like that before. Never.

Bella stood watching her. "Did you have a good time?"

"Yes, thank you, I did," Abigail said, removing her bonnet. "How was business?"

"Slow."

"That's unusual. Usually Saturday is our best day."

"I know."

There was no need to worry. After Wednesday, there would be a decision made, and then the real work would begin. Then she could worry about sales. But until that time, she was going to enjoy this last afternoon with Jack.

"Bella, have you ever been in love before?"

She smiled. "No, but that Jack Turner is a handsome man. Are you in love with him?"

"I don't know. I am certainly developing feelings for him, but I'm not certain." She sat her reticule on the counter and glanced around at the store she was sacrificing so much for. She could be back in Boston, finishing her degree, working for the cause, and meeting with her friends. Yet, this felt like where she belonged.

"As a modern woman working for the movement, do you think falling in love makes us weaker?"

"Oh, no," Bella said. "I think love, with the right man of course, would only make you stronger. You have someone who believes in you, who stands by your side, who encourages you and loves you, regardless of what life throws at you."

Abigail considered her friend's words. "I guess I never looked at it that way, but you would be stronger as a unit, wouldn't you?"

"Yes. Has Jack kissed you?"

"Good Lord, that man's lips are more dangerous than any weapon I've ever seen. When his mouth moves over mine, I almost faint from the sheer pleasure."

Bella laughed. "I've never received a kiss like that."

"Me neither. Those boys in Boston didn't know what they were doing. But Jack's kisses… I can't wait to experience one again."

Bella shook her head and sighed.

"If I fell in love, do you think it would make me appear weak as a person?" Abigail asked, not wanting to give up her dedication to helping women, but knowing Jack was certainly distracting her.

"Good grief, no. Having an entrepreneurial spirit does not make you unlovable or weak. I think we all want to fall in love someday with the right man, get married, and have children. We all want to live the lives of our mothers, just with more control," Bella said. "We want to help make the decisions regarding our welfare and our offspring."

"Yes." Abigail sighed and closed her eyes. "I think I'm falling in love with Jack, but I can't marry him if he doesn't accept me for the woman I am. I just can't. And he has to love me in return."

"Why wouldn't the man love you, Abigail? You're a very interesting woman."

Abigail frowned. Unfortunately, Jack's parents had scared him and made him distrustful of love. And until he overcame that fear, she would never be able to be with him. "Sometimes things in a person's past affects him and causes him to have problems with love."

Bella nodded her head, but didn't question further about why Jack possibly could not fall in love with Abigail. "You would make a wonderful partner for a lucky man. Jack Turner would be blessed to have you in his life."

Smiling at her friend, Abigail couldn't help but think her father's death had changed her life in so many ways, and she missed him more each day. But thank goodness she still had her friends, and they were still fighting for their cause.

And Jack...for the first time in her life, she was interested in a man.

"But will he allow me to continue to promote the women's movement and fight for women's rights? That's the big question."

~

The next night, Jack sat across from Abigail at the same restaurant. Once again, they were drawing the attention of the people in the diner. He could almost see the people leaning in to hear what they were saying.

"Have you had anymore visits from council members?" he asked.

Tonight, she wore a blue gown that accentuated the color of her eyes, making them shimmer in the light of the restaurant. God, this woman was beautiful, smart, and more woman than he had ever dreamed of.

"No, but sales in the store have dropped off dramatically. I think many husbands are telling their wives not to shop at my mercantile, that very soon the problem will be resolved."

"That doesn't make sense to me," he said. "If we make you close the mercantile, where will the people shop? You're our only store within twenty miles."

She shook her head. "I don't know, but business is

slow."

"The city council meeting is coming up on Wednesday. I'm almost certain they're going to vote to shut you down."

She shrugged. "I've already lined up a lawyer in the next town over, and he will have the paperwork ready to file a motion to reopen the store."

Jack sat stunned. This was quickly spinning out of control, and either direction would harm the city he cared about, the one he represented. He'd run for mayor to keep the crazies from taking over and putting even more restrictions on the town, including the desire to shut down the saloon. Tim Barton would love nothing better than to close his business and run him out of town. Just like he wanted to do to Abigail.

"Sounds like you're prepared." But was she ready for the backlash from the townspeople? For the men to be up in arms about her trying to usurp them and the women to meekly follow their husbands? He'd seen retaliation before in this town, and it was never pretty.

The next town over was filled with people who'd for some reason or another garnered the attention of the elite men of New Hope and been escorted to the city limits. He had to try one more time with her.

"It's not too late to sell. That would end all of this, and then you could either start up another store somewhere else, or you could return to that fancy college in Boston."

She bristled at his words. "Why don't you concentrate on selling the saloon? I'm contented to be running my business. I just want to keep it in my family and possibly hand it off to my children. You, you don't even like what you're doing. You're the one who should be selling the saloon and concentrating on doing what you love."

He sat there stunned for a moment. One thing about this woman, she would always be honest with him and tell him exactly how she felt. There would not be any soft peddling from her. "It's because of the exact same reason that you don't sell your business."

"Except, I love the mercantile and you don't love the saloon."

"No. I don't."

"Have you at least considered hiring a manager to run the saloon and then renting out a building for the pharmaceutical company? The town needs both businesses."

He thought about what she'd said. He'd considered hiring a manager and had felt guilty for not wanting to be behind the counter watching. That was the problem with owning a saloon. You had to watch the patrons, watch the bartender, and watch the money flow. You were vulnerable to thieves. "I've considered it, but was always afraid the manager I hired would steal me blind."

"It's a possibility, but we're only given so much time on this earth, and if you don't enjoy what you're doing, then what's the point?" she said, gazing at him with empathy. The woman knew how to reach in and twist his heart.

God, she was so right, yet he hated to give control of his family's business to someone else.

"How much would you charge to rent that room next door to the mercantile?" There he could keep an eye on her and make sure nothing happened. He wasn't certain he would do this, but he'd always dreamed of opening up a pharmacy for the people in town, and this way he could keep the saloon and own the pharmacy. He'd have two businesses to watch over, but at least he'd be doing what he loved.

"I'd let you have it for twenty-five dollars a month."

"I'll consider it," he said, thinking this definitely needed further consideration. "The key is to find a competent manager of the saloon."

"Yes," she said. "I may know someone you could consider, but she's a woman."

He laughed, loving the way Abigail tested him and tempted him as well. "I think that might cause problems. It's against city ordinance twenty-five."

"She's an excellent manager. She tended bar in Boston."

"What?" he asked surprised. He knew some women worked in factories, but letting a woman behind the counter of a bar was like asking a drunk to manage your liquor supply.

"Yes, her mother quit sending her money, so she went to work in the bar for a couple of nights."

Shaking his head, he stared at her. He could solve her problem so easily. All he had to do was ask her to marry him, and if she accepted, the town would willingly let her continue to operate her family business…under his name.

He enjoyed being with her, yet she was different from other women. And maybe that was what drew him to her. When he was with her, he had more fun. They sparred, they laughed, and she made him see life from a woman's perspective. They were both good business owners who could help each other. It just made sense to ask her to marry him.

Never before had he even considered marriage, let alone on the spur of the moment asking for a woman's hand. But suddenly, it was something he wanted more than his next breath.

Gazing at her across the table, he licked his lips, suddenly feeling nervous. He knew how she felt about love and marriage, but still, he hoped she would see the practicality of marrying him. The men of New Hope would be happy. He wouldn't have to run her out of town, and there would be no lawyers involved.

Plus, he enjoyed being with her, and kissing her was

better than any alcohol he'd ever sampled.

He cleared his throat, his nerves rising up and causing his stomach to roil like a ship in a storm. "Abigail, I enjoy being with you. We have fun together, and I think you're the smartest woman I've ever met. We're both good at running our businesses and we enjoy it, but you're in a really bad predicament. And me, I need someone to remind me of what's important in life. I should have already been seriously considering opening up a pharmacy." He took a deep breath, watching her eyes widening. "Would you do me the honor of marrying me? I think we're good together. Your business would be your own. I would never interfere. Together, we would make great decisions. What do you think?"

A frown formed on her forehead as she drew her mouth down. "I enjoy being with you. I've never enjoyed being with a man before now, but I need to know. Do you love me, Jack?"

A lump formed in his throat. What could he say? He didn't really believe in love. He'd never seen the emotion in action between a man and woman. He'd witnessed a mother's love, but not a couple's, and well, he wouldn't start off their relationship by telling her a lie. "I enjoy being with you. I think we're good together, but I don't know if I believe in love."

"So you don't love me."

"I don't believe in love. I don't know what that emotion feels like. I care for you."

She rose from the table, her face an unreadable expression, her lips drawn tight. "Like I've told you, I'm not marrying unless I'm in love and the man returns my love."

"Do you love me?" he asked.

Her face contorted in a painful grimace, and he could see tears welling up in her eyes. Abigail Vanderhooten was not a weak weeping female, yet his words were causing her pain.

"Yes, I was beginning to fall in love with you," she said.

He started to rise and she held up her hand. "No. Please stay. I need the walk back to the store to gather myself."

"I'm not letting you walk home alone."

"I'm not letting you walk me home," she retorted. She dug into her reticule and threw down some bills on the table. "Here's for my part of dinner."

"Come on, Abigail. You're not paying for dinner," he said.

"Oh, yes, I am. As business owners, I won't let another businessman buy my dinner," she said and walked out the door.

His heart sank to his feet, and he knew he was the biggest fool. Why did he feel like he'd just let the best woman he'd ever met walk out of his life? Why did he feel like he'd made a huge mistake? Why did he want to run after Abigail and bring her back and kiss her senseless?

Chapter Seven

As soon as the store opened for business the next day, Jack was at the mercantile. Hell, he'd buy out the whole store, if only Abigail would talk to him. He opened the door and strolled inside.

Bella came out and greeted him. "Good morning, Jack," she said, her voice cold.

Somehow, he had to see Abigail and convince her that even if he didn't love her, they could live together happily. "Where's Abigail?"

"She's busy this morning."

"So she's here and refuses to see me."

Bella smiled. "Yes, Jack, you're right."

With a big sigh, he glanced down at his shoes then back up at Bella. "Tell her I'm not leaving until I speak to her."

"She told me you would say that, and she said to tell you you're only making things worse. Go away. She's not coming out."

He frowned. "You tell her I'll be back later."

Bella shrugged. "She said you would say that, and she wants you to know she will never change how she feels about marrying for love. So, it's best she ends it right now."

Jack felt like someone had carved her initials on his chest or ripped it wide open, exposing his organ to the fresh air. He hadn't expected it to hurt this much if she told him no. He hadn't expected to feel so much pain. "Tell her I came by."

"I will."

He walked out and back down the street to the saloon. He'd forgotten one very important element when he'd asked her to marry him. He'd forgotten she was a naïve girl who believed in fairy tales. He'd forgotten she wanted to marry for love. Now, he'd ruined everything.

~

Bella walked back into the parlor behind the main store. "Did you hear?"

"Yes, I heard," Abigail said. "He doesn't understand."

"You're right, but you're not going to be able to hide from him forever. For one thing you will have to see him Wednesday at the meeting."

Abigail was miserable. Sitting here, listening to Bella and Jack talk, she'd wanted to run out there and tell him it didn't matter. She had enough love for both of them, but she couldn't do it. If he didn't love her now, he never would. And though her heart was breaking, it was better if she let him go.

"I know. But at the moment, I need some time. I need some time to pull myself back together and get over him."

"I'm sorry. I thought he was going to be the man you married."

Abigail blinked away the tears. "I know. I was beginning to believe it as well, but I couldn't do it. After everything we'd discussed, he did the one thing he knew I wouldn't accept. He wanted our marriage to be a business arrangement. I'll go broke before I agree to that kind of life. I've seen way too many women suffer through their marriage when their husbands acquired their wealth."

"Like my mother," Bella said, shaking her head.

"Exactly."

Bella sank onto the couch. "Father said the best business decision he ever made was marrying my mother. And if he could find me, I know he would have the perfect man for me by now. We would join together to form the Bella and Mystery Man Family Trust, and my new husband would have total control over my funds. I don't want my inheritance if that's the only way I can obtain it, marriage to the man of my father's choice."

Abigail sat on the couch next to her. "You ran away from Boston, didn't you?"

Bella's big brown eyes glanced at her sadly. "Yes. I wasn't going to be forced into a loveless marriage. I had to get away."

Wrapping her arm around her friend, Abigail squeezed and released her. "I'm so glad you're here with me. You've helped me so much."

"You're not mad at me for running away?"

Abigail shook her head. "You know better than that. You did what you had to do to keep from being forced into a loveless marriage. Let's just hope your father doesn't figure out where you are."

Bella nodded. "I've been worried, especially if your situation goes to trial. This could be headline news across the country."

A shudder rippled through Abigail at the thought. A long prolonged trial was not something she wanted. But if they insisted on closing her down, then that was what they would get. "I just hope we both don't starve when they close me down on Wednesday. I know that's what's going to happen, and even though I have the lawyer from Mineral Wells coming to the meeting, it will take days, weeks, for him to get the store reopened."

"We'll make it," Bella assured Abigail, patting her on the hand.

"There's some money in Papa's bank account, but who's to say they'll let me near it. And I have some stashed here in the house just in case of an emergency, but it depends on how long it takes to open the store as to whether or not we'll starve."

Bella laughed. "Come on. We're not going to go hungry." She held her arm out and gestured to the room. "We have a whole store full of the ingredients we need to make something, even if it's nothing more than cake."

Abigail giggled. "We'll be fat and broke."

"But we'll be happy," Bella said with a laugh.

A tear rolled down Abigail's cheek. At the weirdest times she would start to cry over Jack. She wasn't backing down or giving up on her ideals.

"Oh, Bella, I didn't know falling in love would hurt so much. I'm in love with a man who has no clue about what he feels. Don't ever experience this feeling, unless you're certain the man wants you too."

~

Jack walked into the mercantile and watched Abigail. She smiled and laughed with Mrs. Fitzgerald, talking about the weather and asking about her children. Jack just wanted the woman to get her supplies and get the hell out of the store, so he could have Abigail all to himself. He wanted to explain to her why he couldn't tell her he loved her, and then he wanted to kiss her and ask her to please reconsider.

Finally, the woman picked up her basket and started toward the door. "Hi, Mayor. I've wanted to talk to you about the spring roundup event the ladies auxiliary is planning."

"Okay," he said. "Why don't we plan on meeting sometime next week after the city council meeting? I'll have some free time then."

"Oh, it won't take but just a minute," she said and went off into a long convoluted spill about what the ladies had planned. All he could think about was getting to Abigail before she disappeared into the back and sent Bella to talk to him. He had so much to say to her and now this woman was interrupting his thoughts and making him forget everything he wanted to tell Abigail.

"That sounds lovely, Mrs. Fitzgerald. You ladies have always done an outstanding job in the past, so I know you will this year as well. I hate to rush you, but I'm in a hurry and need to speak to Abigail."

The woman turned and glanced at Abigail, a suspicious smile on her face. "I'm sorry, Mayor. But we'll talk again, real soon."

"Yes, Mrs. Fitzgerald, we will. Now, if you'll excuse me," he said and hurried toward the counter where Abigail stood waiting.

Dressed in that blue dress he loved so much, she looked absolutely ravishing, yet there was a coldness about her he'd never seen before. She was busying herself at the counter, restocking the candy, and she didn't even stop when he walked up.

"Abigail," he said softly, "we need to talk."

"There's nothing left to say, Jack. You aren't capable of accepting my terms. I'm not willing to give up on my dreams, so there can be nothing between us."

"Abigail, I don't know what love feels like. I care about you. I want the best for you, and I'd always protect you, but I can't promise you love," he said, feeling his chest wrench with a pain he'd never felt before.

She didn't even pause in putting more peppermint sticks into the case. "Those are wonderful sentiments, but unless you can promise me love, we're done. I need the fairytale, and you don't believe in happily ever after. I'm not willing to accept anything less." Standing upright, she barely even looked at him. "What's left to say?"

Shocked at the frosty tone of her voice, he stood staring at her. There had been so much more, but he'd expected his Abigail, not this frigid creature who refused to even give him the benefit of a glance. "You're the only woman I've ever asked to marry me. The only woman I've even considered setting up house with, and just because I can't say those three little words, you refuse to marry me?"

She stopped and turned an icy sapphire gaze on him. "I feel honored you asked me to marry you, but I'm not a woman who must have a husband. When I marry, I want the man I spend eternity with to cherish and honor and love me with all his being, just like I will him. I don't feel you're capable of that emotion. And while I was growing to love you, you couldn't return that love, so we're done."

"But…"

"Good day, Jack," she said and walked back into the living quarters, leaving him standing at the counter, staring after her.

He felt the urge to hit something, to knock it to the floor and smash it to pieces, but he knew that would never gain him her favor.

So instead, he slunk out the door, wishing with all his heart he'd never asked her to marry him, and that his Abigail was once again smiling at him, teasing him, and challenging his way of thinking.

~

Jack wiped down the bar again. It was way early, and there were very few clients in the hall so far today, but he couldn't sit still. He couldn't sit and think about how he'd taken a leap of faith without thinking everything through, including the fact that she wanted the fairytale.

Hearts and flowers, cupids and arrows, rings and cake, and probably a white gown as well. This woman wanted him to care about her, and sometime soon, she was going to realize there was no such thing as a fairytale romance. That was something they'd created in order to get people to tie the knot. His brother was the closest person to having a happy marriage that he knew.

His brother. It had been months since Jack had seen Luke. He threw down the rag, calling back over his shoulder to his bartender. "Take care of things. I'll be back."

Within an hour, he was sitting across the table from his

brother, while his sister-in-law fixed them lunch. "I need you to be honest with me."

"What?" his brother asked. "You come riding in here like there was something wrong. I was afraid the town had turned against you. I've been hearing rumors of you having problems with a mercantile owner."

Jack shook his head, not ready to talk about the case with his brother. Instead, he wanted to know if Luke was in love. "When you met your Sarah, how did you know you were in love with her?"

Luke glanced toward the kitchen, where his wife was cooking, a smile coming over his face. "She wouldn't see me any longer. Told me she had decided not to see me because I was not serious in pursuing her."

"Were you chasing her?"

"I wanted Sarah, but her family was difficult, and I didn't want to provide her father with financial proof I was a good man for his daughter," he said matter-of-factly like there were no emotions involved. This was Jack's younger brother, the cool efficient man who rarely smiled and seldom laughed.

"He required you show you had money to marry his daughter?"

"Yes, the old man said his daughter would not be a pauper or that any man she married would take advantage of her. Her old man was protective of Sarah, and I can't blame him."

Running his hand through his hair, Jack tried once again to learn the answer to his question. "But how did you know you loved her?"

Luke smiled and shook his head, his eyes clouding over like he was stepping back in time. "She saw my hesitation at providing what her father wanted and told me that if I couldn't do what her father asked, then I didn't want her. Then she told me never to come around again. We were done."

He glanced toward the kitchen. "I was crazy about Sarah, but that made me angry, so I decided to give her up." He laughed. "Within two days, I'd brought her father everything he'd asked for and was back in front of her on bended knee asking for her forgiveness and her hand in marriage. Thank God, she said yes. It's been the best decision I ever made. Those two days were the worst days of my life. I realized I'd lost her forever. "

Jack shook his head. "It's just that after Mom and Dad's marriage I don't know if I ever want to get married."

"Our marriage is nothing like theirs. I don't think Sarah would put up with some of the stunts that Papa pulled. I'd find myself coming home to my things thrown out in the yard and her telling me to get on down the road. And I'm glad because it shows me how much she respects herself and what she wants from me," he said, smiling at Jack.

"So, when you couldn't see Sarah, you knew you loved her?"

"I thought things were over between us, and I was miserable. The thought of never seeing her again, of never being able to hold her and kiss her was enough to make me realize I was a better man with her in my life. I knew I loved her."

Jack sat back. Hadn't Abigail made him a better man? Wasn't he miserable without her?

"So, what's going on with you, brother? You look like you did when you were a boy and ate too many cookies. You look miserable."

"Abigail made me see things differently. She's shown me new points of view and made me rethink some of my outlooks about life. And, Luke, I *am* absolutely miserable. I asked her to marry me, and when I couldn't tell her I loved her, she said no."

Luke gazed at his brother. "Sounds like a smart woman.

We don't think love is important until we don't have it, and then we realize just how much we need that loving touch that smile from a woman and the feel of her arms around us. Sarah is a wonderful woman who makes me see my world in a different light. I don't think I'd be happy without her."

Jack sat there, his heart breaking. He was such a stupid fool. Abigail had caused him to regret making a vow to never fall in love with her. And then he'd ruined everything when he'd asked her to marry him, but couldn't confess his love. One way or another he had to make this right.

"Thanks, Luke. You've given me some insight, and I think I know what I've got to do. Somehow, I've got to show her I love her, and I think I know how."

Chapter Eight

Abigail, Bella, and Mr. Thurston, the lawyer from Mineral Wells, slipped into the back of the city council meeting, hoping they wouldn't be noticed. The place was packed with men from the town. Of course, several heads turned in their direction, but what would they do? Stop the meeting and ask them to leave?

They were late because they'd had to first go through at least twenty-five women who were standing outside shouting, "Repeal the bill."

Every woman had stopped Abigail and wished her luck, told her to be strong and not to back down. Tears had streamed down Abigail's cheeks at the support these ladies had shown her.

But now she had to face the worst, the decision making process of the New Hope city council.

Tim Barton was talking. "Gentlemen, the founder of our great city, my great-grandfather specially had the law drawn to exclude women from owning a business, having a bank account, owning property, or being able to vote. Women are to follow their husband, do his bidding, and not strike out on their own. When a woman comes of age, a father should find a suitable husband for his daughter, and if he has business interests, he should leave them to her husband. As much as I liked Walter Vanderhooten, he should have planned accordingly for his daughter. I recommend we continue with our current laws and take Miss Vanderhooten's business from her and send her out of town."

Some men in the crowd clapped.

George Potter stood up and took the floor. "How many women have we had in this town who've had their husband die and leave them destitute or with children who needed raising? I can think of at least four women in my lifetime, but how many since old man Barton founded the town? Not everyone has a family they can fall back on, and these women were hard workers who just wanted to support their families. I think it's time we rescinded these laws and made it possible for women to earn a living."

Abigail's heart warmed toward the man who had so elegantly defended her position. Not all men wanted this silly law. Just the ones who felt threatened by women and change.

After several more men stood up and spoke, Jack rose before everyone and took a deep breath. "A month ago, I would have laughed and probably written the order to close the business and have Miss Vanderhooten run out of town, even though I admired her father and the business he built." He paused and paced the floor in front of the room. "I know for a fact Miss Vanderhooten has obtained a lawyer and is ready to fight this battle to the highest court in the land. In her words, the law is archaic, outdated, and she just wants to retain her birthright."

There was a murmur in the crowd as the men realized there would be a lengthy, costly court battle.

Abigail kept looking down at her hands clenched in her lap. Her heart was breaking as she watched Jack up there talking about her as if they meant nothing to each other. She loved this foolish man who wouldn't recognize an emotion if it were a rattler and bit him.

"As your mayor, I like to look at all of my options. We could stand firm and try to keep women from owning a business, but how much is that lengthy court battle going to cost the citizens and are we prepared for such a bitter fight?" He paused and let his words sink in.

He was a really good orator and had the men in the room listening to his every word.

"Are our town folk willing to pay more to live in this city while we combat this fight?" He walked along the front of the room. "So, I went to the surrounding towns to see how they handle women-owned businesses. I visited three towns, and all three had no laws against women owning a business. I found at least five businesswomen. I spoke to the mayors at length about what problems the town has encountered because of these female entrepreneurs. They laughed at me and said they were some of the best businesses in town."

Again, the men murmured amongst themselves, and Jack waited for them to quiet before he continued. "I'm a single man. And during my investigative probing, I spent quite a bit of time with Miss Vanderhooten. We had dinner a couple of times. I went to her business; she came to mine."

He shook his head, and the men laughed. "We went to look at some property I'm considering buying, and I found her to be a quite charming young woman. She's forward thinking, and in the future, I think all of our young women will be outspoken, determined, and wanting to feel like they don't have to depend on a man to take care of them. It's imminent, whether we like it or not."

Murmurs filled the room again. Jack waited and then finally held up his hand.

"Why don't you just marry her and solve the problem?" one of the men said out loud.

Jack hung his head for a moment, and then he looked at the crowd. "I tried. I asked her to marry me. Not to solve the city's problems, but because she's a wonderful woman. But she said no."

"Let's run her out of town then," another man yelled.

Holding up his hands, Jack said, "No. That's what I'm here to tell you. If you want me to resign as your city mayor, I will, but I will never shut down this woman's business or run her out of town. I realized too late, but I've fallen in love with Abigail Vanderhooten."

Abigail gasped, drawing Jack's attention to her sitting in the very back of the room with her lawyer and Bella.

He walked toward her, and the men's heads turned to watch him. "As I stand before you now, don't expect me to shut her down."

The room fell silent as he stopped in front of her. "I love you, Abigail. I didn't know what that emotion felt like until you told me no. Since then, I can't eat, I can't sleep, and all I can think about is the time we were together. I miss you."

He dropped to one knee, and she gasped again, placing her hand over her mouth as tears flooded her eyes. Her lungs seized, and her heart pounded rapidly in her chest. Jack, her Jack, was asking her to marry him.

"I'm a better man because of you. I now know what it feels like to love. For the rest of my life, I will honor you, cherish you, and stand beside you, even when you march in defense of women. I'll be there until I take my last breath. Will you marry me, Abigail Vanderhooten?"

With a sob, she pulled him up to face her and threw her arms around him. "Yes, I'll marry you. I love you and I just needed to hear you say those words."

"Thank God," he said. "I missed you so much. I thought I'd lost you forever."

"But I'm not giving you my business," she whispered against his shirt. "I'm still going to want my independence. I'm still going to march for women's rights."

"Honey, I'd be disappointed in you if you didn't continue your fight. I don't want your store. I'm working on plans for the pharmacy," he said softly to keep the others from hearing. "I'll be busy enough with a wife and two businesses and maybe some babies."

She laughed and looked up at him in surprise. "Children? We never talked about children before."

"And we will later," he promised.

She stared at him, uneasiness suddenly coming over her. She bit her lip and then asked, "And what about my friends who are coming? Are you going to run them out of town?"

He smiled and said quietly in her ear, "Oh, my little freedom fighter. You are definitely going to keep my life interesting. No, honey, I'm not going to run them out. I'm going to stand by your side and welcome them, but let's not tell these men about the other women just yet. Let's wait until the council accepts this new provision."

The men clapped as Jack and Abigail came apart, and several stepped up and gave them congratulations.

Tim Barton ran to the front of the room. "It's wonderful you're getting married, but I'm calling for you to resign as mayor. This has been mishandled from the start, and that business should still be shut down."

Abigail resisted the urge to march up there and kick that man's shins until they were bruised and bloody. She watched as her fiancé walked up to the man.

Jack smiled and nodded at the troublemaker. "Tim, I know you hated losing to me as mayor. But why do you want to ruin Walter Vanderhooten's business and give his daughter so much trouble? It's his legacy. Why? Let's do a vote right here in this room. How many want to take this fight to the Supreme Court and continue not to let women own a business?"

Two hands went up. Tim Barton and Sam O'Brien. All of the rest of the city council remained silent.

Jack smiled at Abigail. "On that motion, ordinance fifteen has been officially defeated. Women may now own businesses in the town of New Hope, and Miss Vanderhooten's store will remain open." He turned to look at Tim. "As her future husband, I will take offense to anyone who misaligns my wife. Good day, gentlemen."

Abigail waited as Jack walked through the crowd,

shaking hands and accepting the congratulations of many of the men. She'd found her man. The husband she'd wanted, but never thought she'd have, and together the two of them in the upcoming months were going to change this little town into a mecca, where women would be welcomed with open arms. And hopefully her friends would also find men right here in town they could fall in love with.

Jack reached her side and took her by the arm. "When can we get married?"

She smiled at him. "I think a political leader like you needs a big event. And my friends will be here in just a couple of weeks. Can you wait that long?"

"You're testing me," he said, pulling her into his side. "I love you, Abigail, and it feels so good to say those words."

She rubbed her hand along his cheek. "It feels good to hear them, Jack Turner, and I can't wait to be your wife. Abigail Turner, women's rights defender."

Thank you for reading!

Dear Reader,

Thank you so much for reading *Abigail: Scandalous Suffragette.*

Whether you loved the book or hated it, I would appreciate it if you let everyone know by leaving a few words on your favorite vendor's website.

If you enjoy western historical authors, please join the Pioneer Hearts group on Facebook. This is a fabulous group of readers and authors who enjoy westerns.

Sign up for my newsletter at sylviamcdaniel.com if you'd like to learn about my new releases as soon as possible.

Reading one of my books is like spending time with me, and I just want to say thank you from the bottom of my heart.

Yours in Drama, Divas, Bad Boys, and Romance!
Sincerely,
Sylvia McDaniel

Books by Sylvia McDaniel

Contemporary Romance

Standalones
The Reluctant Santa
My Sister's Boyfriend
The Wanted Bride
The Relationship Coach
Her Christmas Lie
Secrets, Lies, and Online Dating
Paying for the Past
Cupid's Revenge

Anthologies
Kisses, Laughter & Love
Christmas with you

Collaborative Series

Magic, New Mexico
Touch of Decadence

Western Historicals

Standalones
A Hero's Heart
A Scarlet Bride
Second Chance Cowboy

The Cuvier Women
Wronged
Betrayed
Beguiled

Lipstick and Lead
Desperate
Deadly
Dangerous
Daring
Determined
Deceived

Scandalous Suffragettes
Abigail
Bella
Callie
Faith

The Burnett Brides
The Rancher Takes a Bride
The Outlaw Takes a Bride
The Marshal Takes a Bride
The Christmas Bride

Anthologies
Wild Western Women
Courting the West
Wild Western Women Ride Again

Collaborative Series

The Surprise Brides
Ethan

American Mail Order Brides
Katie

About the Author

Sylvia McDaniel is a best-selling, award-winning author of historical romance and contemporary romance novels. Known for her sweet, funny, family-oriented romances, Sylvia is the author of The Burnett Brides, a western historical western series, The Cuvier Widows, a Louisiana historical series, and several short contemporary romances.

She is the former President of the Dallas Area Romance Authors, a member of the Romance Writers of America®, and a member of Novelists Inc. Her novel, A Hero's Heart, was a 1996 Golden Heart Finalist. Several other books have placed or won in the San Antonio Romance Authors Contest and the LERA Contest, and she was a Golden Network Finalist.

Married for nearly twenty years to her best friend, they have two dachshunds that are beyond spoiled and a good-looking, grown son who thinks there's no place like home.

She loves gardening, shopping, knitting, and football (Cowboys and Bronco's fan), but not necessarily in that order.

Look for her the first Tuesday of every month at the Plotting Princesses blogspot, and be sure to sign up for her newsletter to learn about new releases and contests. Every month a new subscriber is entered into a drawing for a free book!

She can be found online at: www.sylviamcdaniel.com or on Facebook. You can write to Sylvia at P.O. Box 2542, Coppell, TX 75019.

Recently married Layla Cuvier is awakened to the shocking news that her husband is murdered and that she is not his only widow. It's true, she hated Jean Cuvier who forced Layla's father to sell his shipping company and sanctioned their marriage. There may be three Cuvier widows, but Layla is the most likely suspect to his murder.

Forced to turn to the man she blames for the sale of her father's shipping company, she must trust Drew Soulier, the best attorney in New Orleans. Layla knows that Drew doubts her innocence and is only using her trial to further his political ambitions, yet she can't seem to deny his allure and finds herself struggling to resist her desires. Is Drew the man to find the truth that saves Layla from hanging and heals her troubled heart? Or will he stop at nothing to achieve his goal to be mayor?

Sneak Peek into Beguiled

New Orleans, 1895

Sunlight glittered through the windows of the St. Louis Hotel, casting bizarre shadows over the dead body of Jean Cuvier. A sparrow trilled a happy song in the courtyard outside the posh hotel suite, the sound eerie and disturbing. Layla Cuvier stared at the corpse of her husband lying on the floor and knew that from this day forward, her life would forever be changed.

No longer will I have to endure his touch.

Her eyes confirmed what Colette, her servant, had told her. Jean lay sprawled on the floor, his brown robe wrapped around him, his face a peculiar shade of pink. Needing the confirmation of what seemed so obvious, she reached down and touched his hand. The feel of cool flesh beneath her fingers sent a shudder through her and she recoiled in revulsion.

"Mrs. Cuvier, a doctor is on his way and the hotel manager has sent for the police," said Colette, wringing her hands in an anxious manner.

Layla felt numb as she stared at the man she had shared a house with for the last year. As his wife, she should feel sorrow at his death, but relief and a sense of peace filled her. She had barely tolerated Jean's presence.

She rose and nodded to her servant and friend. "Please help me dress before the doctor arrives."

"Of course," the maid said, but glanced at her hesitantly.

"Did Mr. Cuvier say anything about feeling ill?" Layla asked, gazing at her husband's still form.

"No. But I went to bed before you retired," the maid said. "Did you hear him call out?"

"After I shut my bedroom door, I heard nothing last night," Layla said, knowing the sleeping draught had ended her insomnia. The draught created a dream world filled with people and color, and a world so different from reality. Yet she would have heeded Jean's call if she had heard his cry for help. "So many nights he slept in the chair."

And Layla loved the nights he left her alone.

"It's so sudden. How do you think he died?" Colette asked.

"I don't know. He hasn't been ill." Layla gave Jean one last glance, stunned at his death. Their last conversation was an ugly reminder of his evil ways and she couldn't help but wonder if his heart could have failed him. Though their marriage had been a farce, she had never expected him to die. "Let's hurry. I'd rather greet the authorities fully dressed."

"Are you all right?" Colette asked gazing at her worriedly as they entered Layla's bedroom. "You seem so composed."

Layla gave the woman a quick glance as she shed her nightgown. "I'm a little shaken, yet I feel strangely calm."

Calm and relieved, she hoped that now his ugly secrets would die with him and she could escape this farce of a marriage and return to her home.

Hurriedly Layla chose a black dress appropriate for a widow. She had barely gotten her ebony hair swept up off her neck in a coiffure that left wisps of curls swirling around her face when Colette opened the door to the police. They swarmed into the suite, covering the rooms like a bevy of ants.

Layla stepped out of her bedroom, and into the doorway of Jean's bedroom to watch with interest as a uniformed policeman leaned over Jean's prostrate body lying on the floor.

The voices of the officers seemed distant and removed and the scene before her surreal, like a colorful nightmare.

A short ugly little man dressed in a shabby brown suit separated from the others and walked toward Layla.

"Mrs. Cuvier?" he asked, his intimidating eyes focused on her.

"Yes?" She felt as if he stared deeply into her soul, but she had nothing to hide and met his gaze, undaunted by his beady gaze.

"Detective Dunegan of the New Orleans Police."

They walked the short distance to the lavishly decorated parlor of the suite.

"Please sit." She pointed to a chair in the small sitting area as she sat across from him.

"How did your husband die?" he asked. He took out a notepad and a pencil from his tattered coat pocket.

"I don't know. My maid awakened me this morning with the news that she'd found Mr. Cuvier lying on the floor of his bedroom. I hurried into his room, where I found him lying there, his body already cold," she said, clenching her hands in her lap. "I have no idea how long he's been dead."

Layla glanced toward the bedroom, half expecting Jean to walk through the door, laughing that he had fooled them all.

"When did you last see him alive?" the detective asked.

She thought back to the night before. They had fought fiercely and she had been determined to return home to Baton Rouge this morning. She had intended to meet with an attorney to see what kind of legal recourse was available to her, but miraculously nature had taken care of things.

Now she prayed the ugly truth would die with Jean and she could return to her previous life. She licked her lips nervously.

"The last time I saw Mr. Cuvier was around midnight," she said, remembering how she had left him in the parlor asleep in the very chair the detective occupied.

A man stood in the doorway to Jean's room with a stethoscope hanging around his neck. "Detective Dunegan, can I speak with you a moment?"

Through the open window, she could hear laughter in the courtyard of the hotel, the sound incongruous with the atmosphere in the suite.

The two men disappeared into the bedroom. Their muffled voices held an excited undertone, though she could not understand what they said. As the minutes passed, she sat feeling more nervous, wondering whom she should contact regarding Jean's death.

"Now where were we?" he asked. "Oh, that's right. You said the last time you saw the deceased was around midnight." He paused and frowned at her. "Did you and Mr. Cuvier sleep in separate rooms?"

"Yes. My husband kept odd hours, and I have trouble sleeping and don't like to be disturbed."

"So, you heard nothing in the night? He didn't call out to you for help or assistance?"

"No, I took a dose of a sleeping draught not long after he came home." She gave the detective a puzzled glance. "Do you always ask these kinds of questions when a man dies?"

"I'm just doing my job, Mrs. Cuvier," he said matter-of-factly.

"No, I took a dose of a sleeping draught not long after he came home." She gave the detective a puzzled glance. "Do you always ask these kinds of questions when a man dies?"

"I'm just doing my job, Mrs. Cuvier," he said matter-of-factly.

Layla glanced around and noticed that more and more policemen seemed to be filling the hotel suite. They stood around in little clusters talking, occasionally glancing in her direction. A few of the officers seemed to be combing the room as if they were looking for something.

"What are they doing?" she asked alarmed. She had never heard of the police doing this when someone died.

The atmosphere seemed charged with some ominous foreboding that she didn't understand.

He ignored her question. "How would you describe your marriage to Mr. Cuvier?"